"Hi," Dav
bed, his ha
deeper than

Laney felt tongue-tied. He nearly glowed with life. "Hi, yourself."

His lips twitched. "Not very eloquent, are we?"

"No," she whispered.

David hesitated. "It's strange," he finally said, "but I missed you." It was even stranger that he was saying the words. As soon as he'd arrived home, he'd run up the stairs to see her.

"I missed you too." She paused. "Where are your boys?" Laney asked hesitantly, trying to break the tension.

"Mabel's feeding them cookies. I told them I would bring you down. Want to go?" he asked.

Yes. No. Yes, she wanted him to hold her. No, she wanted to stay here alone with him. The attraction between them was stronger than ever. Finally, she nodded. "David?"

He smiled at the sound of his name on her lips. He closed the door and in a few short strides he was there beside the bed, carefully sitting down on its edge, so close she could touch him.

She didn't want to, but she couldn't help it. Her hand reached out and rested on his thigh. His hand clasped hers, and her fingers tightened, warming his hand, warming her heart. Then he leaned down and brushed his lips over hers, and she sank into a sweet quicksand of warm honey. . . .

WHAT ARE *LOVESWEPT* ROMANCES?

They are stories of true romance and touching emotion. We believe those two very important ingredients are constants in our highly sensual and very believable stories in the *LOVESWEPT* line. Our goal is to give you, the reader, stories of consistently high quality that may sometimes make you laugh, sometimes make you cry, but are always fresh and creative and contain many delightful surprises within their pages.

Most romance fans read an enormous number of books. Those they truly love, they keep. Others may be traded with friends and soon forgotten. We hope that each *LOVESWEPT* romance will be a treasure—a "keeper." We will always try to publish

LOVE STORIES YOU'LL NEVER FORGET
BY AUTHORS YOU'LL ALWAYS REMEMBER

The Editors

Patricia Potter
The Greatest Gift

BANTAM BOOKS
NEW YORK · TORONTO · LONDON · SYDNEY · AUCKLAND

THE GREATEST GIFT
A Bantam Book / January 1992

*If you would be interested in receiving protective vinyl
covers for your Loveswept books, please write to this address
for information:*

Loveswept
Bantam Books
P.O. Box 985
Hicksville, NY 11802

ISBN 0-553-44192-2

Published simultaneously in the United States and Canada

PRINTED IN THE UNITED STATES OF AMERICA

OPM   0 9 8 7 6 5 4 3 2 1

One

David Farrar glared at the message in his hand and expelled a long, heavy sigh of frustration. The last thing in the world he needed.

A reporter named Lane Drury from Washington was at the decaying hotel in Cade's Valley, the small community David called home, and wanted an interview.

David swore under his breath, low enough so his son wouldn't hear. Damn the man. He hadn't even extended the courtesy of calling and asking whether David would consent to an interview, apparently assuming that an article would be welcomed.

It wasn't. The kids—his students—and their families would suffer, would feel like objects of charity, the one thing they resented above all. The people in this valley had little but pride, but they had that in generous quantities.

"Hey, Dad, we're all out of bows."

David looked down at his youngest son who was already destroying the order Mabel, his occasional housekeeper, had brought to the house. Within five minutes of arriving home from school, Theo was already up to his neck in Christmas wrapping paper.

David couldn't help but grin at the disaster that spread out before him. Boxes were everywhere, as were scraps of gaily decorated Christmas paper, ribbons, and tags. Gertrude's small black head pushed out above the mess; a huge red bow had fallen over one of the dog's blind eyes, giving her a clownish look.

"Perhaps if you used them for packages instead of for Gertrude . . ." David told his son.

"But Mabel said some reporter is coming, and I wanted Gertrude and Henry to look their best. They sorta looked raggedy last time."

"They *are* raggedy," David stated. "And the reporter won't be here long enough to notice." He would make sure of that.

Theo's face fell slightly. "I think it's awesome seeing our picture in the paper."

David leaned down and brushed a lock of hair from his eight-year-old son's face. "You think everything is awesome," he said gently. He cherished his happy-go-lucky son who still pitched in so enthusiastically with wrapping packages, even after weeks of doing so every afternoon and weekend.

His older son, Abe, often escaped to his room after putting in what he considered a fair amount of hours. It wasn't a lack of compassion or interest on Abe's part. Eleven going on thirty, Abe simply needed time to himself as much as he needed air to breathe. He had always been that way, quiet and thoughtful and diligent in his studies, while Theo was barely contained dynamite, full of energy and enthusiasm and mischief. He had a grin that lit the world, and an "ain't life great" outlook. David earnestly hoped he would never change.

David was so lucky to have these two boys, to have a job he loved in a place he loved. He only wished that Julia could see their sons now.

David dropped the note in his hand and leaned down to untie Gertrude's bow. She reached up with a wet tongue to indicate her gratitude.

Gertrude was a kisser. She had been wearily trotting down a country road when David and the boys had first seen her. She had been nothing but bones, but she'd found enough energy to give David a swipe of the tongue on the neck, an unfortunate expression of affection she'd continued.

And then there was Henry, who was probably someplace under all this paper. Henry was another stray dog that somehow managed to make its way to the Farrar household. Animals had uncanny instincts in spotting a patsy, David thought frequently. That's why their household also included a three-legged cat, a rabbit adopted after one of Abe's friends said his father threatened to eat him, and a hamster from a school project. Strangely enough, they all tolerated one another, as if they understood this house was a sanctuary.

The next step was natural, David realized—he had adopted an entire school. Julia had always said he never knew when to draw the line.

And now a reporter threatened the trust he had so painstakingly built.

He would not allow it to happen, he vowed. Dammit, he wouldn't.

Annoyed at himself for his anger, he turned his attention to Theo. He needed to cool off. "Why don't you take Henry out for a walk? I'll get my coat and join you."

"Great," Theo said. Neither snow nor sleet daunted him. He loved the outdoors. "I'll race you outside."

"Your coat and hat and gloves," David warned.

Theo nodded and dashed to the hall closet, while David hurried to his bedroom.

• • •

If Lane Drury didn't hate clichés, she would have said Bah, humbug. She satisfied herself with a more modern condemnation of fate and circumstances as she stared bleakly out the car windshield, trying to see through the sleet splashed against the glass.

Every mile of this godforsaken trip had been a nightmare. The roads had been icy and treacherous and cold drizzle had greeted her every time she'd stopped to stretch her legs. She was tired and discouraged and angry.

Very, very angry. Mostly at herself.

She had brought this upon herself, though she'd tried to blame Patrick Simon, her editor. She knew deep within that Patrick had been right when he'd said she had not been doing her best work.

But a Christmas feature! She thought she had moved beyond that long ago, moved to the highest level of her profession. And that made her humiliation over her present assignment more acute.

She peered out the window, seeking house numbers but none of the five houses on the street seemed to have any. The hotel proprietor had not been very exact in his directions; she'd already made two wrong turns before realizing that her guide's idea of what comprised a street was far different from her own. Like everything else in Cade's Valley, nothing seemed organized or efficient.

She gazed to the right. It had to be the house on the end. Crates were all over the yard, and an old pink pickup truck sat in the driveway. Pink, for Pete's sake. She'd never seen a pink pickup, but it figured. Somehow, it figured.

The house itself looked like a picture from a storybook. It was a large two-story structure with a big front porch complete with swing and rocking chairs.

She slowed down, looking for a place to park, when a boy and a dog came sprinting out the front door.

The dog dashed in front of the car, and the small boy yelled and ran after him. Frantically, she jerked the steering wheel to the left and automatically stomped on the brakes although she knew that was the worst possible thing she could do.

The car skidded, just barely missing the boy and dog, and went into a ditch. Her head hit the windshield as the car landed with a tremendous crash, and everything went dark.

"Daaaad . . ."

David heard the long scream and the steady blaring of a car horn and raced to the door. He recognized the panic in Theo's voice. Something calamitous must have happened, for neither of his boys were alarmists. They'd been through too much.

Outside he saw Theo kneeling in the middle of the driveway, clutching Henry while the dog howled. Across the street the rear end of a car was sticking up out of the ditch at a thirty-degree angle.

"Are you all right?" he asked Theo.

Theo nodded and clutched Henry tighter. From the noises Henry was making, David quickly figured that he, too, had escaped unscathed.

David moved as quickly as he could across the slick, icy street to the car. The ditch, used for drainage, was several inches deep with water and covered by a thin layer of ice. He ignored the cold water seeping into his loafers as he climbed down to the driver's side. Only one person was in the car, a woman he'd never seen before, and she lay motionless across the steering wheel, stained by several drops of blood.

He rapped on the closed window, but she didn't move. He tried the door, but it was jammed.

David went around to the other side and found that door locked and the window rolled all the way up. He knocked on the windshield, but the woman showed no sign of hearing him.

Because he didn't smell gasoline, he dismissed his first thought of fire. But his heart pounded as he considered other possibilities: concussion, internal injuries, shock. Fear such as he hadn't felt since his wife had been diagnosed with cancer streaked through him. Guilt, too, since he had little doubt the accident had occurred because of his son and dog. He was all too familiar with that emotion; it kept him awake at nights even two years after Julia's death.

David yelled to Theo, "Tell Abe to call Sheila Morrison—the number's beside the telephone—and ask her to come over quick. Then bring me a hammer and towel."

Aside from the nurse, there was no one else for him to turn to. Cade's Valley no longer had a town government—it couldn't afford one—and the area was served by the state patrol whose nearest station was more than fifty miles away. So was the nearest hospital. The lack of medical services had kept him away all the years Julia had been sick, and for the first time since he'd arrived here from Boston after her death, he questioned his wisdom in doing so.

David looked back inside the car. He tried to see if there was any color in the woman's face, but long, straight mahogany-colored hair hid it from view. He could only deduce from the hairstyle that she was fairly young.

What in the devil was she doing on this street anyway? It led off the main road and ended abruptly at a field that was no longer farmed. The only reason she would be here was if she was coming to see him.

But he wasn't expecting anyone. Except a reporter named Lane Drury, and he'd assumed Lane Drury was a man. The woman couldn't . . . Just as he was about to check the license plate, Theo appeared at the top of the ditch, holding a towel and hammer. As David was reaching for them, he saw his closest neighbors, Sam and Sarah Talley, approach. Sam took one quick look into the ditch before dropping down beside David.

"I'm going to break a window," he told Sam.

He chose the rear right-hand one, so the woman wouldn't be showered with shards of glass. He sure as hell didn't want to cause her more injury. He tapped the window with the hammer until it cracked. Using the towel to push the glass in, he reached inside and unlocked the front passenger door. It opened easily. He slid onto the seat, cut the ignition off, then felt the woman's pulse. Her skin was soft, the fingers long and slender, like those of a pianist. The heartbeat was strong and steady, thank God.

He was afraid to move her until Sheila arrived, but he gently brushed her hair back. There was a small cut on the forehead, along with a goose-egg-size bump. Even though her face already showed signs of swelling, she was one of the prettiest women David had ever seen.

Her skin was ivory, and long black lashes framed her closed eyes. Her lips were nicely sculpted and looked as if they smiled easily. Her cheekbones were high, her chin strong and determined. The hair felt like silk and smelled like fresh flowers. David couldn't help sliding his fingers through the strands.

She moaned, and he moved closer to her.

"You're going to be all right," he murmured. "You're going to be fine. Just stay still."

He could see her trying to open her eyes, her lashes

fluttering before the lids revealed slivers of dark eyes. Her lips barely moved. "The boy . . . "

David's heart sank. She *had* gone off the road because she'd been trying to avoid his son. He owed her a great deal.

"He's fine," he said softly.

"And . . . the dog?"

"You're the only casualty," he replied, trying for a light tone as he watched the eyes open completely. They were a very dark brown, and there was pain and confusion in them, and also relief—for his child and the animal. He felt an immediate liking for this woman, who thought of others before herself.

She tried to shift and gasped, her hand going to her leg.

"There will be someone here soon to help," he said. "Don't try to move until then."

"Who . . . ?"

"I'm David Farrar," he answered. "The boy you swerved to miss is mine. I owe you thanks as well as apologies."

"I'm . . . just glad he's . . . all right." She closed her eyes and swallowed hard, and David had enough experience with pain to recognize it.

He took her hand and held it tightly, feeling her fingers close around his as a drowning person's might. Despite her injury, the clasp was strong and warm, and a sudden surge of electricity ran through him. He fought burgeoning feelings of protective-ness, of tenderness, feelings he didn't want again, feelings he couldn't afford again. He steeled himself against such emotions, but she looked so vulner-able. . . .

She was saying something again, and he leaned closer to hear the words. "Darn Patrick, I knew this was—"

He never discovered exactly what she knew, because his attention was grabbed by the distinctive sound of Sheila's Jeep pulling up.

"What do we have here?" Sheila's calm voice questioned.

David gently freed his hand and a strange sense of loss filled him as her fingers slipped from his. He got out of the car and explained the situation to Sheila.

She slid inside. "How do you feel, honey?"

David, leaning over, saw the woman attempt to smile. "I'm trying to figure that out," she said weakly.

"Can't be too bad, then. Can you move your hands? Good. Your feet? Try moving your head slightly."

David clenched his teeth as the questions went on. He knew enough about first aid to realize that there was no major back or neck injury, but he heard the gasp of pain when the woman tried to move her leg.

He saw the apprehension on Sheila's face and it didn't help the guilt and sympathetic pain he was feeling. He looked toward Theo, and his face was also furrowed in anxiety and self-blame. Some of David's anger faded. Theo anguished over the demise of a fly; he would need no further punishment than to hear the woman's groan.

Sheila straightened up. "I think her leg's broken. I'm going to fasten a temporary splint, and you and Sam can take her inside. But she has to go to the hospital for X rays. I just don't know how bad it is. Once we have her warm inside, I'll call for a helicopter."

Sheila gently raised the woman's leg and stretched it across the seat, then went to fetch the splints from her Jeep. No sound had come from the woman, but her lips had tightened with concentration, and her eyes glazed over with pain. He wanted to comfort her, although he sensed a control and reserve about her that kept everyone at a certain distance, even now. Unexpectedly, he felt a gnawing need to penetrate that reserve, while at the same time internal warning voices screamed at him. *Not again! Not ever again!*

"God, I'm sorry about this," David said. "If there's anything I can do, Miss . . . "

Her eyes, which had been half closed, opened slowly, regarding him with a wry resignation that for some reason struck him as touching.

"Is there someone I can call?" he added.

She seemed to consider the question, and then shook her head.

"Are you sure?" he persisted.

"I'm sure," she replied with finality, and then her eyes closed again as if answering had taken all her strength.

David moved away when Sheila returned. He saw the woman's lips tighten once more with pain as the splint was fastened, and then she shook her head as if to dispel any weakness. A curious aching and admiration filled him at her quiet gallantry.

When Sheila was finished, she helped the woman across the seat toward the open door, and David reached down, picking her up carefully.

She was slender and light, and the feel of her body next to his revived longings best forgotten. But he couldn't avoid smelling the light, flowery scent of her, or being affected by her wary, guarded expression.

As his arms tightened around her, their eyes met, and he felt a spark ignite between them, the kind of magnetic recognition that rarely but magically flared between two people, two strangers.

David tried to brush the sensation away. He had no intention of getting involved with a woman again, particularly a woman such as this one: distant and obviously successful, if her clothes and car were any indication. He had learned a hard lesson. He was finally getting his life sorted out, and he and his sons needed nothing as much as peace and stability in their lives.

Her dark eyes wrenched away from his face, as if she, too, were feeling that sense of connection. Perhaps it was only because he felt responsible for her. He prayed it was.

At any rate, he told himself as he crossed the icy road, she would be gone soon. A helicopter would drop from the sky and spirit her away as quickly as she had appeared.

But a reluctance to give her up streaked inside him, and he pressed her closer to him as he mounted the two steps up to his porch and waited for Theo to open the door.

David's gaze caught hers again, and her eyes were like a well into which he could so easily fall. He saw the startled realization in hers, and her hand clenched his shoulder.

"No," she whispered, and shook her head as if denying the attraction that was so immediate and so strong between them.

"No," he agreed with such emphasis that her lips puckered in confusion before she turned her head away.

Inside, Abe was frantically clearing the sofa of boxes and paper. David quickly laid her down, as if he wished to rid himself of something burning him.

He stepped back, almost trembling as her eyes searched his face with an intensity that scorched him. And then the light seemed to dim, and again he felt a terrible sense of loss that sent shivers through him.

Two

Laney stared around the room with a reporter's eyes.

Despite her best intentions, they kept returning to the man whose arms had held her so confidently. She had never been carried before, and she was surprised at how comforting it felt, how the warmth of their bodies met and meshed, how pleasant the proximity was.

But such feelings were the last ones she wanted to experience.

David Farrar. The man she'd been sent to interview. Dammit all. She wished he weren't so darn tall as he stood above her; he had to be at least six feet two. His expression was a study in contradictions, showing both concern and wariness. She also detected confusion, which she sensed was rare in a face that was so strong, almost craggy, with deepset eyes, thick, golden brows, and stubborn chin. Lines stretched from his eyes, and she wondered whether they came from laughter or trouble. She wondered why she cared—and was confounded when she realized how much she did.

His eyes were moss green, and his hair sandy-colored. Wet from the snow, it fell to the collar of a light gray shirt barely visible under a deep green Irish knit sweater, and needed a cut. One unruly clump hung over his forehead.

She watched as he impatiently brushed back the damp clump, to no avail. It simply fell forward again, and she heard his resigned sigh, her heartbeat increasing its tempo slightly at the sound.

David Farrar was a very attractive man. And he was nothing like the man she'd conjured in her mind. For some reason, she had envisioned a bespectacled, slight man who taught in a small rural school because he didn't have the ambition or talent to do anything else. She had, she thought guiltily, composed such a portrait because she resented this assignment.

David Farrar defied every one of those preconceptions. He was obviously a strong man, both physically and in other ways. A lively intelligence sparked in his eyes, and determination and character were etched in his face.

Laney didn't want to see character. She didn't want to like him. She didn't want to be attracted to him. She had been fooled before, betrayed before by a handsome face, by what she thought was integrity. She wouldn't believe in it again. Ever.

She couldn't afford to waste time; too much was at stake. Her career was at stake.

So she tried to take her mind from the man and the pain and looked around the room.

It was currently awash with paper and packages, some wrapped and some only in their boxes. A large, well-worn leather chair was covered with bows and ribbons. The furniture was a mishmash of styles; some pieces were quite elegant while others looked like handcrafted country: a rocking chair, pine bookcases filled with hardcover and paperback volumes, another chair beside a table piled high with magazines. An old model television sat on a rickety stand. There was no VCR or electronic gear.

Despite the clutter, she had the impression of warmth, of a house well loved. She thought of her own apartment—a high-rise two-bedroom with a balcony overlooking the Potomac—and realized how it resembled all the motel rooms she'd stayed in. Colorless, indistinguishable. But, she reminded herself, it was only because she hadn't had time to make it a home yet; she'd been too busy.

Suddenly she remembered her car.

"My car," she managed to say, resisting the urge to look up into David Farrar's face. Instead, she kept her eyes on the woman who had splinted her leg, who was now talking on the phone in a low voice.

In one easy motion, David Farrar swept aside the clutter on the end of the sofa and perched on the edge of the cushion. "Don't worry about anything. I'll see that it's taken care of."

His voice was a deep rumbling baritone, and he had a peculiar accent. Some words were drawled; some carried a New England inflection. Whatever it was, it sang of self-assurance. Why did a man like him hide in a small, poverty-ridden valley in West Virginia? He looked more lumberjack than teacher, more soldier than succorer. Except for his eyes. Kind eyes. Wise eyes. Wary eyes.

Laney had never seen any quite like them before. They were magnetic and drew her gaze. But she must break their hold, so she moved slightly, knowing that pain would follow. She welcomed it as a diversion.

His voice gentle and reverberating through her like the compelling purr of a big cat, he asked, "Did I hurt you—bringing you in?"

She shook her head, not trusting herself to speak. She didn't want his sympathy. There was something about him that screamed for her to keep a distance. She'd had enough of magnetic men.

And where was his wife? Surely there had to be a wife if there was a son. For some ridiculous reason, the notion caused another ache that, she feared, had no relation to her physical injuries. She looked around again.

She saw few feminine touches. The curtains were plain, utilitarian. There were no knickknacks or dried flowers.

Her reporter's aggressiveness failed her. She had a natural shyness that she'd learned to subdue, but now it seemed to overwhelm her once more.

She closed her eyes, and felt his hand on her arm. She forced herself to tense, and she felt his quick withdrawal as if he sensed her confusion. Damn. He was her subject, her interview, her quarry. Now she was at *his* mercy. Laney felt shivers climb up her back. She'd had a premonition from the first moment this assignment had been forced on her.

Patrick had told her to write a story on a rural schoolteacher, "a special one," he had said, "who'd been able to coax corporations all over the country to give his kids a real Christmas." It would make "a great Christmas Day feature," he'd added, "what with all the concern over education and good teachers."

It was the kind of thing that Laney used to excel in, but she'd worked her way up to covering presidential campaigns, and this seemed too humble an assignment. Nothing less than punishment.

She'd known she hadn't been doing her best work. She was recovering from a disastrous romance, and she was burned out from the campaign trail, but it was only temporary.

Patrick's insistence made her all the more determined to win the job she had been seeking, that of Washington bureau chief for a national magazine.

Then she would be making the decisions. She would finally have the independence she had been working so hard to obtain.

And now this. She almost grinned as she remembered an old saw: Cheer up, things can be worse, and sure enough she cheered up and things did get worse.

She opened her eyes, willing the last hour to have been only a nightmare. But he was still there, kneeling beside her like a knight. And the throbbing in her leg was worse.

His expression was even more worried than earlier. "Are you all right. That bump . . . "

She shook her head. "I was just thinking of something."

"There has to be someone I can call," he insisted again.

No," she said. She couldn't call Patrick and tell him she'd failed, that she couldn't do one simple feature. She had friends, but they were more than several hundred miles away, and she didn't feel she could impose on them. There was no one, no one who could do anything. From the time she was thirteen, she'd taken care of herself and her mother until her mother died. She would do it again now, but for the first time the prospect was bleak, and that bleakness turned into anger against the man next to her. If it hadn't been for the damned story, this never would have happened. And yet she had a stubborn core of honesty that told her this was all her own fault.

That knowledge didn't help, though. Instead, she grew angrier when she remembered her response to his arms. She still felt it: the tingling, the sparking of nerve ends. What right did he have to make her feel that way? she thought illogically.

She looked up at him accusingly, and saw him wince.

"I'm sorry about Theo and Henry," he said. "I take full responsibility."

"Theo and Henry?" she echoed, confused.

"The boy and dog," he replied patiently. "I'm grateful you swerved to miss them. Henry means everything to Theo, and Theo means everything to me."

"Which is the boy and which is the dog?" Laney said with irreverent humor.

He grinned, and his eyes lit up like leaves of a tree when the glint of sun hit them. Darn, Laney thought, he was even more attractive when he smiled and laugh lines creased around his eyes.

"Sometimes I wonder," he replied with the same offbeat humor.

"But," he continued, "Theo's the boy and Henry's the dog, and right now they both belong in the same place—the doghouse."

Some of Laney's discomfort faded, although all her warning flags started flying. He had a dangerous smile, so irresistible, she found it impossible not to respond. It could coax the proverbial bird from the tree, she thought.

Dean Kelly had the same kind of smile, and she knew how much that one was worth. She fought to take her eyes from David Farrar.

Damn. She didn't want to be here. She hadn't wanted to be in his arms; she didn't want to be in anyone's arms. She had kept her distance from men since she had told Dean Kelly exactly where he could go.

She didn't like feeling this man's strength, nor smelling his light scent of soap, nor knowing the warmth of his body. Most of all, she didn't like feeling so dependent, so helpless.

All of that must have shown on her face, for she saw his expression change, saw a cloud move over his eyes. She nervously shifted under the gaze.

Pain arched up from her leg, and she couldn't stop the slight moan that escaped her lips. She heard his indrawn breath.

"I'm sorry," he said. "So sorry." His voice held regret and sincerity, also a promise of safety and warmth.

She had once thought Dean represented safety and security, and she was never going to be foolish enough again to believe in appearances, in surface emotions.

Her thoughts were interrupted by the approach of a young boy, the boy who had run out into the street. His face was a study in misery.

David Farrar stood and put his hand on the boy's shoulder. "This is Theo," he said.

The boy hesitated, looking as if he was trying desperately to hold back tears, then moved closer. He had cornflower-blue eyes and a blond cowlick, and his lips were trembling. "Henry and I are very sorry. We didn't mean to hurt you."

Laney felt very sorry for him. "Of course you didn't," she said. "I'm just glad you . . . and Henry are all right."

"Henry wants to thank you," the boy said, and all of a sudden Laney was aware of a wet nose sneaking up above a sofa cushion while a bushy tail thumped anxiously. Henry was, she thought with a smile, a great white hairy combination of breeds with eyes as anxious as Theo's. She could almost swear that Henry was apologizing. Or perhaps he always wore that needy look.

"You're welcome, Henry," she said solemnly, and shook the proffered paw with dignity, winning still another smile from David Farrar, one she wasn't sure she wanted. It did too many strange things to her. A second dog, a small black mutt, bumped into Henry, looked puzzled for a moment, then reached out a wet tongue to show affection to everything and everyone within range.

Laney was beginning to feel overwhelmed.

"That's Gertrude," David Farrar said, laughter in his voice. "She's blind, but she believes the way to happiness is universal love."

"Is that a way of telling me she's indiscriminate, that I shouldn't be flattered?" Laney retorted, that uncontrollable humor popping out again. It always did when she was uncomfortable, unsure. It was her flip way of covering uncertainty.

"At the moment, I would call her very perspicacious," he said with a half smile.

"What's per . . . perpic . . . percacious?" Theo asked.

"Per-spi-ca-cious." David Farrar pronounced the word slowly for his son. "It means lucid, perceptive. You know what perceptive means?"

"Yeah," Theo said with a broad grin. "It means smart."

"Pretty close," his father said, and Laney was warmed by the obvious affection between father and son.

"Theo, why don't you take Henry and Gertrude upstairs, and then make our guest a cup of cocoa. For you and Abe too," he said.

"But Henry wants to get better acquainted," the boy complained.

"Which really means," his father explained, "that Theo wants to get better acquainted."

Just then another boy came into the room, an older boy whose serious face was made even more so by thick glasses. Behind him sauntered a three-legged cat which rubbed itself against Theo's leg, its head tipped as if to ask why Laney was here. The room suddenly seemed to swim in color, in animals, in boys. Laney felt like Alice in Wonderland, and she shook her head to make sense of things. She was usually very good at bringing order out of confusion, of analyzing a situation and placing it in proper perspective.

But that ability deserted her now. She was speechless, unable to think, to reason, lost in a cacophony of sound and impressions and feelings and pain. Although she hated herself for doing so, she looked up at David Farrar with a plea in her eyes.

His mouth softened and he looked so impossibly appealing that Laney's heart lurched. Then she felt herself shiver. She didn't think it was for physical reasons until she saw the immediate frown in David Farrar's face. She glanced down and noticed goose bumps covering her hands.

"Get a blanket, Abe," he told the older boy. "And Theo, take the animals into the other room." His voice held a no-nonsense tone.

Theo still hesitated. "But—"

"It's all right," Laney said. "I don't mind."

"Then what about that hot chocolate?" David Farrar said, concern etched all over his face. "I think Theo wants to do something."

She shook her head. She wanted to leave. She felt vulnerable here, and she had vowed never to feel that way again, never to leave herself open again.

"Is there anything else we can get you?"

She shook her head.

David sighed, feeling more and more responsible, yet thinking the last thing he needed was an appealing and lovely woman in his life. And despite her bruises, she was definitely beautiful, with her lustrous mane of hair and huge brown eyes. They were clouded with confusion and uncertainty, but he suspected they were usually clear. And her quick humor, her refusal to call for any help, told him she was probably used to being in control.

Once more he wondered who she was and why she was there. With the confusion, he had not thought of asking.

"Why," he said, "were you on this road?"

She didn't have a chance to reply. Sheila had turned to them, her face grim as she said, "There's been an accident on the interstate up north. The helicopter isn't available and may not be for some time. We need X rays of that leg, and also of that bump on her head. I would drive her to the hospital, but apparently Billie Allen's been trying to get me. His wife is in labor, and I have to get over there." Her eyes turned to David. "Can you take her?"

David didn't hesitate. "Of course. I'll call Mabel to look after the boys."

Sheila nodded. "Use my Jeep. We can prop her up in the backseat, and it has snow tires. I'll take your truck."

David knew the offer was a measure of Sheila's concern. She protected that Jeep as a mother protects a child.

"I'll take good care of both of them," he said.

Sheila looked out the window. Night had fallen and light sleet was making white streaks in the black sky. "I don't like this weather."

David didn't either, but he didn't see many choices. If they waited much longer, the weather might make the roads impassable, and if the accident upstate was serious, there was no telling when they would get assistance.

"I *am* here," the woman said suddenly, and both David and Sheila turned to her. "You're talking about me as if I'm a child, or one of those dogs or . . . something," she said with asperity. "Don't I have anything to say about this?"

"You're right," David Farrar said, grinning abashedly, which immediately calmed Laney's irritation. She moved, as if moving would prove there was nothing wrong with her. But she couldn't restrain a moan as agonizing pain spread through her leg. "Damn," she said, biting her lips against further outcry.

David arched an eyebrow at her. "Any other suggestions?"

"Than riding in a Jeep on a mountain road in an ice storm?" she returned dryly.

Sheila went over to her, placing a reassuring hand on her shoulder. "David's an excellent driver. Otherwise I wouldn't entrust Dragon to him."

"Dragon?"

"My Jeep. It sort of sounds like one." Sheila smiled. "Don't worry, I would never let you go if I weren't sure you would make it. But you need help for that leg, and I've done everything I can."

Laney stared helplessly at the two people waiting on her. She wondered how she would get home, how she would complete this darn assignment, and how she would get around and run after stories if the leg was broken.

But she had no choice. It was ridiculous not to follow the suggestion of the two people before her, even though she didn't know them. Still, the idea of putting herself into the hands of a complete stranger, of a man, was devastating.

She finally nodded.

Sheila looked relieved. "I can't give you anything for pain, not until a doctor checks that bump on your head," she said. "But we'll make you as comfortable as possible. The trip shouldn't take more than two hours."

Two hours! A lifetime, Laney thought, but she was

silent as the room swung into motion. At David Farrar's orders the two boys got plenty of blankets and an armful of pillows and took them out to the Jeep. Sheila made another phone call and told the hospital to expect a patient.

Another person appeared at the door, a weathered woman with a kind face and lean body. She introduced herself as Mabel, who served as housekeeper and baby-sitter. Pale blue eyes regarded Laney with sympathy, and then turned to David.

"You go right ahead, and don't worry about the boys or the time," Mabel said. "I'll stay here as long as I'm needed."

The man nodded and grinned. "You're a gem." He looked down at the boys, his gaze lingering on Theo. "We'll talk about this tomorrow," he said. Theo winced.

David Farrar leaned down and picked Laney up, making sure the blankets were wrapped tightly around her. She felt his warmth and strength, and yielded to the comfort it offered. She didn't want to, but there was something so gentle and soothing about his touch, and she was so tired and hurt so damned much.

The top of the Jeep had been buttoned down, and a mountain of pillows nestled in the rear seat. She was carefully settled down among them, her leg propped up and cushioned. Sheila Morrison took one final look, and nodded before shutting the door.

The Jeep started, and a rumbling noise that made Laney think of an awakening dragon filled the interior. Laney felt lost in a dark world filled by the sound of sleet against canvas, the grumbling of a complaining motor, and the tangy odor of after-shave lotion. The scent relaxed her. Somehow she knew the man in front would take care of her.

The thought was both reassuring and very troubling.

Dammit. She didn't want anyone to take care of her. She didn't need anyone, Not for long, anyway. In a few hours he would be gone and she would be back in control.

And that was exactly what she wanted.

Three

Both driver and passenger were silent for a long time.

David concentrated on the increasingly hazardous road, and Laney on ignoring the growing pain and stiffness. Every bone in her body seemed to cry out in misery from the not-so-smooth ride.

She tried not to think of what her prognosis would be. She wanted to get through this assignment and then return to the campaign trail. Dean would be there, of course, and that would make things awkward, but she couldn't allow him to believe he was important enough to sidetrack her career. She was well on the way to the culmination of a professional goal, and she wasn't going to allow anything—or anyone—to interfere.

But the prospect of going back to the job she had left didn't fill her with the excitement it once did. She was thirty years old and she was tired of trying to find new angles on the same speech, an illumination of a candidate who was all charisma and little substance.

Laney had been a workaholic since she was a teenager and had taken a job to help out her mother. They had never had a house, only a cheap apartment, and even that had been a struggle to keep.

Laney had always wanted so much more, and she'd worked hard for it, waitressing while in high school and in college, where she'd earned a four-year scholarship. She had hoped that after she graduated, she would be able to take better care of her mother, but Bethann had died one month before Laney's graduation, and Laney had been all alone.

She had substituted work for family, pouring all her talent and energy into her job. She had started with a large regional paper, then was hired by *The Washington Times*. Instead of dating, she accompanied other reporters on their stories, learning everything she could.

Political reporting was considered the top of the ladder in her profession, and she found she was very good at it. She had a disarming smile and manner that often made underlings and assistants, even top officials, say more than they intended. On the national beat, she covered minor congressmen, scoring some surprising scoops, and quickly moved up to cover more important figures, until she finally won a prime assignment on a presidential campaign.

She loved the first few months: the traveling, the camaraderie, the jokes and pranks. And she fell in love, or thought she did. She now suspected it was the proximity and the way they lived: different hotels each night, drinking sessions that often lasted late into the night, competition that collided with friendship. She often woke up trying to remember what city she was in, and what time the plane left for what other city.

It was a situation ripe for romance, with reporters away from home for weeks and months at a time, with so many empty hours to fill, so much pressure to produce fresh and original copy, to score against one's friends and colleagues.

So for the first time in her life, she'd allowed her

heart to become seriously involved, and it had been a disaster.

"Are you asleep?"

David Farrar's voice was low, so as not to disturb her if she was, indeed, asleep.

Laney thought about pretending she was, but she felt the need for human companionship, for the sound of someone else's voice. The sleet had turned into hail; she could hear it pounding against what seemed a fragile covering above them.

"No," she replied softly.

"Are you comfortable?"

Laney decided to be honest rather than polite. "Not particularly. How long before . . . ?"

"Another hour, perhaps more," he said. "Should I stop and do anything for you?"

"No." She just wanted to get there, to reach a resolution of some kind, to know what lay ahead of her, even while she dreaded knowing. She had felt the same way when her mother had had a stroke. She had to know what she would be dealing with, even when the knowing was so painful.

David Farrar's words broke into her memory. "I still don't know your name."

"Laney," she said.

"Laney?"

"Lane Drury. I'm the reporter who contacted you."

She saw his shoulders stiffen, and she wondered why. Most people, if they hadn't just been indicted or arrested for some crime, enjoyed being interviewed, especially those involved in charitable endeavors. Publicity usually brought in more money. And the *Times* had received a press release about David Farrar and the project for his students. Having grown suspicious after nearly ten years as a reporter, she wondered whether David Farrar had something to hide. Was he an impostor, a charlatan?

It seemed ridiculous after seeing the house full of those scruffy animals and his two boys. Yet she was not imagining the hostility that had just invaded the Jeep.

"You did get the message about an interview?" she asked.

"I don't remember a request." The words were said in a terse, hard tone she'd not heard before. And the warmth was gone.

The Jeep ran over a jut in the road, and the resulting bump made her cry out in pain.

"Sorry," he said. Some concern was back in his voice, yet the warmth was still missing.

Puzzled, she decided to probe. "You don't like reporters?"

"I don't care about them one way or another," he said bluntly. "But I don't want my students exploited."

His coldness and determination chilled Laney. Her own back went up. "We received a news release. That usually invites attention," she said, her tone as icy as his. She didn't like being called an exploiter of children.

"I didn't write the damn thing."

"Someone did."

His shoulders, which had grown even more tense during the exchange, suddenly relaxed. "I'm sorry," he said slowly. "I shouldn't blame you, but if you'd called . . ."

"I tried," she said. "No one answered." And she had been impatient to get it over with. So she'd sent a telegram, believing he would be only too eager for the story.

He released a heavy sigh. "I owe you, Miss Drury. God knows, I realize it's my family's fault you've been hurt, but my kids . . . their families are very proud. There never should have been a press release. Publicity takes away some of the magic for these kids. I've been able to explain to other reporters who've called. . . ."

Laney had never heard a man speak that way, of magic for "his" kids, who were not his kids at all. She wasn't used to such compassion; reporters were, by and large, a cynical lot, and they had been her sole companions for years.

Silence settled uncomfortably between them. Laney wished she could say she would forget the story, but she couldn't. Patrick had made it a matter of pride, and she'd never begged off an assignment. Broken leg or not, she would see this one through. David had said he owed her, and she would use that if she had to. She would also make sure that her story didn't hurt anyone.

She leaned back and gazed away from his broad shoulders, the thick sandy hair that curled slightly, and recalled the strength of his arms when he'd carried her. He didn't seem like the type of a man who would choose to teach, particularly in such a poor area.

He had an air of sophistication and a take-charge demeanor that bespoke a high-powered executive. His speech was more exact, more clipped, than others that she'd heard in the community, and his boys seemed to have a Massachusetts accent.

David Farrar was a mystery, an enigma. Perhaps there was more than one story here.

He would not welcome her interest, but she'd always found ways to get people to open up to her.

And he did owe her.

She closed her eyes, trying to forget the past few hours and how they might affect the next few weeks and months. Senator Paul Tribling would start campaigning again on January 10. She already had a seat reserved on the press plane. If she wasn't there, someone else would get it, and she might be assigned to more features. Unless she got the bureau-chief job. But the competition was tough.

As she shifted slightly, pain rushed through her once more. Dammit, she thought. How could so many things go wrong?

David pulled up in front of the small community hospital. It was brightly lit, the parking lot full of ambulances and movement. He hoped the emergency room was clear enough to treat his passenger soon. He looked at his watch: ten o'clock. Even if he left now, he wouldn't be home until after midnight.

But he knew he couldn't leave Lane Drury there alone. He would probably have to spend the night at the motel across the road. Mabel, he knew, would take good care of the boys.

He got out and moved the seat up. Lane had finally gone to sleep, and in the lights of the hospital he could see her bruised face. He felt a sudden ache for her, for her defensiveness that he sensed hid vulnerability. He wondered at the fact that she'd given him no names of relatives or friends to call. Certainly someone as attractive as she would have someone who cared about her, who would want to know she was injured. Perhaps even a husband. He didn't particularly care for that idea, even while he understood how foolish the reaction was.

He touched her gently, and her eyes opened, puzzled at first and then widening as she realized where she was. "The hospital?"

"We made it," he said, leaning down to her. "You stay here. I'll get some help."

As he entered the hospital, its personnel were moving quickly in and out of cubicles, and the reception area was filled with people. A frazzled-looking woman sat at the front desk.

"I have an accident victim in my car. Sheila Morrison called in."

The woman's expression became even more harried. She looked down at a paper in front of her. "The broken leg," she said. "I'll call an orderly and gurney, but it will be some time before a doctor can get to her. They're all busy . . . an accident on the interstate . . ." The phone rang and she turned away.

Frustration knotted David's stomach as he waited several minutes. An orderly finally appeared, and David led him to the Jeep. Together they placed Laney on the gurney and wheeled her to a place along the wall.

David was summoned back to the receptionist's desk.

"Insurance?" the woman asked.

"I'll ask, but if not, I'll guarantee the bill."

The woman eyed him warily. "Are you a relative?"

He shook his head.

"Friend?"

"Not exactly."

She studied him with weary eyes. "Then what, may I ask?"

"Would acquaintance do?" David said with exasperation.

The woman raised an eyebrow. "Just have the patient fill out these forms."

David looked down at all the questions. He'd filled out enough hospital forms in his life to be an expert. He hated the way they reduced people to lines on a page, just as he hated the smell of a hospital.

He'd always known the answers with Julia, but now he knew only two of them—Lane's name and her occupation.

He walked over beside her gurney and leaned

against the wall. "There are some questions . . ." he told her.

Thirty minutes later he was surprised at how many she'd answered and yet how little he knew about her.

"Relatives?"

She shook her head. "None?"

"Friends?"

She'd hesitated before reluctantly giving two names.

"Insurance?"

"Yes, the paper has excellent insurance. My card is in my purse." When she realized she'd left the purse in her car, David saw the sudden panic.

"Don't worry," he said. "Sam will take care of it. Cade's Valley isn't Washington, D.C."

"But—"

His hand settled on her shoulder as she tried to raise herself up. "But nothing. We'll take care of anything that's needed. Just give them the name of the insurance carrier, and I'll call Sam later for the number. Okay?"

It wasn't okay. Laney felt her life suddenly being controlled. But she didn't know how to protest without sounding ungrateful and foolish. She nodded.

But it still wasn't okay.

He finished the forms and still stood there, and Laney felt very uncertain. She must look a mess. She'd felt a sizable bump on her forehead, and her face was probably swollen. Her hair hadn't been brushed since the accident and she didn't have a trace of the lipstick she'd put on before leaving the hotel for David Farrar's house.

He, too, was disheveled, but he still looked attractive. With his sheepskin jacket and wind-tousled hair, he reminded her of the Marlboro man. Then she noticed that he eyed the hospital halls warily. She received the instant impression that he didn't like being here any more than she did.

Laney decided to come to his rescue. "Thank you for driving me, but there's no reason for you to stay. I can take care of everything myself."

She probably could, he thought, but he didn't want her to. Despite her reason for coming to Cade's Valley, he felt responsibility and something he hadn't felt since the early days of his marriage: a curling warmth in his belly. "What about the story?" he asked.

"I—I'll call you."

He shook his head. "I'll wait here and see what the doctor says. Theo will want to know."

There was something very cold and lonely about a hospital, and David Farrar's presence gave it a warmth she needed at the moment. All the same, the feeling warred with an equally vital desire to be strong on her own.

"Your sons . . ."

"Mabel has stayed with them when I had to be out of town," he said. "They'll be fine."

Laney wished a doctor would come right away, wished something would happen, wished that she didn't feel a need for the man who stubbornly stayed with her. She closed her eyes, but even then she could see those concerned green eyes, the furrowed brow, the rugged, handsome features. She recalled the love in his voice as he had spoken to his son, even when he had scolded him for running out in the road, and she thought how much she had missed that kind of affection when she was a child, especially from a father she had wanted to have. She had started then to learn from her mother not to trust men. And she hadn't, not until Dean. That had been the biggest mistake of all.

She was once more struck by the absence of a

Mrs. Farrar. Oddly, that observation gave her some comfort, although for the life of her she couldn't imagine why. Neither did she understand why she tingled all over every time David touched her, accidentally or on purpose.

Nor why their eyes so often locked together in a battle of wills . . . and something else, like the joining of two energy fields. Nothing else seemed to describe the electrical currents that flowed between them, especially when they were so close.

She would be back in Washington shortly, and she would forget the entire episode. So why did she wonder about Theo's mother?

David Farrar returned the forms to the desk and sauntered back with a half smile. He leaned against the wall once more, seemingly relaxed although his shoulders were tense. He was gazing toward the examination rooms as though willing a doctor to come, and she saw his face in profile. The enticingly shaped lips smiled easily, and the lines at the corners of his eyes crinkled. She couldn't see his eyes now, but she recalled them in her mind. They were so . . . well . . . stunning in their clarity. She'd never seen eyes quite that color before, and they fascinated her.

Her thoughts were suddenly interrupted by a doctor who hurried over, apologizing for the delay and ordering an aide to wheel the gurney into a private cubicle. She was examined, taken for X rays, then examined again. Finally she heard the news that the leg was indeed broken and needed surgery to be reset.

She was prepped and given a shot of something that made her sleepy. As she was being rolled down pale green corridors, she saw David Farrar walking beside her, a reassuring smile on his lips. Suddenly she felt much better. In fact, it was frightening how much better.

• • •

It was three in the morning when the doctor entered the waiting room. David was half asleep, sitting on a leather couch that had seen better days, but he woke instantly as the surgeon looked toward him.

"How is she?"

"It was a serious break. She'll be in pain for a few days, and she needs to be off the leg for several weeks. She might be ready for a walking cast in a month. I don't think there's a concussion, but she needs to stay here at least twenty-four hours for observation. She'll have some bad bruises on her face and a real shiner." He hesitated. "We're way over capacity because of the interstate pileup. We might have to transfer her to a hospital in Charleston unless she has friends or family who can care for her at home."

"She doesn't need a hospital?"

"It's not necessary."

David inwardly winced. He remembered that damned form. Relatives: none. And he remembered her refusal to call anyone.

"Can she travel in a Jeep?"

"How far?"

"Cade's Valley."

The doctor's smile relaxed. "Sheila's territory."

David nodded.

"We'll keep her today, take more X rays tomorrow morning, and if everything looks okay, she can leave Sunday," the doctor said. "I'll give her something to ease the pain along with instructions for Sheila."

David nodded, thinking of the implications of his decision. He had more than enough room, and Mabel could stay over and care for her. It would be for just a few days, until she was well enough to get back to Washington on her own. God knew, he owed her that much. It could have been Theo in the hospital.

But he couldn't stifle pangs of doubt. Laney Drury was altogether too appealing, and the last thing he needed was another ambitious woman. He also knew that staying with him would give her the opportunity to do the story he didn't want told, that he was afraid would destroy the tenuous bond he had built with people already suspicious of outsiders.

But he didn't have a choice. None at all.

Laney found out about the arrangement half a day later. She didn't have a choice. None at all.

She'd woken in a strange bed, in a woozy state of mind, and with a dull ache in her leg, which she suspected would be much worse when the drugs wore off. She'd sipped ice water when the doctor appeared, along with David Farrar, and quietly listened.

Laney wanted to go home, to the apartment that she'd never really used, to the emotional security that her private cocoon provided. She was loath to impose upon David Farrar, whose mouth was grim and whose eyes said he wasn't sure about the situation either.

Laney turned to him. "Are you sure . . . ?" she asked, hoping he would say no, but he smiled instead, as if he knew her thoughts and sympathized. She wished he weren't so darn appealing, especially that morning, with his hair obviously combed by his hand, his clothes wrinkled, and a light beard stubbling his cheeks. Most men, she thought, would have looked worn and ragged. Perhaps the shot she'd just had made her mind totally fuzzy.

That made her more susceptible to agreeing to almost anything. The following day she would probably regret it.

But right then, as she looked into his eyes, she couldn't say no.

Four

"Good afternoon." The deep, low voice pierced the fog still clouding Laney's world.

Laney heard the words and turned her head toward the tall figure in the doorway, and wretchedly remembered everything that had happened in the past twenty-four hours.

Her visitor wore a smile that was meant to be reassuring, but Laney felt only confusion and a quickening of her blood. He had shaved and looked more rested than he had early that morning. Every attractive line of his face was outlined in the stream of sunlight flowing from the window, and his eyes seemed to penetrate her every thought in a way no one else had been able to do. Her heartbeat accelerated, and she tried to attribute it to anything other than the man himself: the injury, the shock to her system, the painkiller she'd been given just moments earlier.

His mouth crooked in a particularly appealing way that held reserve and natural friendliness, as if he didn't quite know what to expect from her. It was an expression that dug into her heart and prompted a slight, unwilling smile of her own.

Laney frantically attempted to restore her defenses. She didn't want to feel warmth for this man, for any man. So she tore her eyes from him and looked around. Her bed had been crowded inside a small room already holding two patients, reminding her only too well of the overcrowded condition of the hospital and David Farrar's offer.

And her acceptance.

Hesitantly, because he seemed to be waiting for a reply, she thought of the weather, the time-honored subject of nonpersonal conversation.

"Is it," she replied hesitantly, "a good afternoon?"

"Glistening," he said, his smile growing wider as if to dispel her doubts. "Cold, bright, and glistening."

She shivered, and not entirely from the thought of cold temperatures. Watch out, she told herself. Remember Dean. He also had a heart-quickening smile and enchanting eyes.

But he'd never had David Farrar's warmth, or the crinkling laugh lines around the eyes that indicated he embraced the world. Again she wondered about him, why he was in a small West Virginia community when his confidence told her he would be comfortable almost anyplace.

"Are you sure about my staying with you?" Laney hoped he would say no. She would find some other solution. If there was one thing she was, it was inventive. Also enterprising. All her life she'd been finding ways to get where she wanted to go.

Only this was different. She didn't want to go where she was obviously headed. But she had agreed, and part of her wanted to go with him. That fact worried her more than anything else. "I'm sure," he answered.

She finally asked the question that had been plaguing her. "Your wife . . . ?"

The smile fled from his face. "She died two years ago."

Laney felt unaccustomed awkwardness. She was used to asking questions. Her business was asking questions. But right then she felt as if she'd pried into a place she had no right to go. "I'm sorry," she said softly.

Part of a smile returned. "No need," he said. "It was a while ago."

"Still . . ."

He shook his head and held up a bag. "I bought a few things for you. A toothbrush, toothpaste, comb, some lipstick." He hesitated, looking uncertain for the first time. "I didn't know what shade."

Somehow the idea of rough-hewn David Farrar searching for lipstick was touching. That he even thought of it was more endearing.

And then she realized she probably looked like something the cat dragged in from the woods after a particularly stormy night. Her hand went to a limp strand of dark hair that fell over her hospital gown.

"I've never seen anyone look so good in one of those," she heard him say, a touch of amusement making it lilt, and she swore silently at herself for being so obvious.

She shouldn't care what he thought. But still his comment planted a tiny seed of warmth.

She reached out and accepted the package he held out to her. "Thank you," she said a little shyly. "I have some luggage at the hotel in Cade's Valley."

"I'll ask Sam to fetch it," he said. "In the meantime I guess we'll have to get you something to wear on the way back." He eyed her plaster-encased leg. "I doubt if your slacks will go over that cast."

Laney looked down at her shapeless hospital gown and winced. Her one suitcase was filled mostly with slacks she couldn't wear now. She had lost suitcases before on planes, had worn the same outfit for several days, but the lack of clothes bothered her now as it never had before. She didn't want to be dependent on this man for everything. She wanted to face him on equal ground.

His eyes quickly examined her, and Laney felt naked under a measuring gaze that seemed to penetrate the gown and send sizzling heat through her. "Size ten?"

It was an accurate guess. He obviously knew women's sizes and Laney felt an odd sense of jealousy. She nodded somewhat ungraciously.

"Red, I think," he said with another appraising look.

Again the correct assessment affected her oddly. Red was her favorite color, and the most flattering one. "Anything," she said shortly. "I'll reimburse you."

He shook his head. "No," he said. "I think shopping for you will be a pleasure. Don't deprive me of it." The words were accompanied by a mischievous smile as if he were anticipating a particularly delightful day. Laney tried to remain rational. He felt guilty, she knew, although he shouldn't. She was the one who had put herself in this mess, first by letting her personal life interfere with her professional one, and then by losing control of the car.

"Your sons . . . how will they feel about an unexpected guest?" she asked, changing the subject.

"I've asked them. They're delighted. They like reporters." There was a slight emphasis on "they."

She raised an eyebrow. "And their father?"

"I think we've already discussed that."

"Not entirely. I was under a disadvantage."

"Somehow I don't think you're ever at a disadvantage." There was no barb in the tone, only a wry observation.

Laney wished that were true, particularly now. He made her feel tongue-tied and awkward. His eyes were too knowing, his presence too mesmerizing, his smile too dazzling. She didn't like the weakness that had nothing to do with the accident, that had everything to do with his presence.

"And you?" she tossed back. "Are you ever at a disadvantage?"

He laughed then, and Laney thought she'd never heard such a fine sound. "With a classroom full of children? Often."

"Why did you become a teacher?" That was the question that had been pounding at her.

"That's a long story."

"Will you tell it to me?"

He shrugged, the gesture a negative answer.

"Please," she coaxed.

"Why?"

She was used to asking the questions, not answering them, and she didn't know how to answer that particular one. She suddenly knew how her subjects sometimes felt. It was a disconcerting feeling.

She reverted to cool professionalism, a façade she had perfected. "It might make a good story."

"Is that what everything means to you? A good story?" His smile was gone now, his eyes cool as he leaned against the wall. But despite the relaxed pose, she saw the rigidity in his body.

Her eyes searched his, wondering at his change of mood. She thought about answering a defiant yes, but before she could utter it, a doctor was entering the room, a cheery smile on his face.

She had never felt quite so uncheery in her life, especially as David Farrar slipped out the door. The room lost a certain glow.

Laney wasn't given much time to think about his absence. The doctor checked the cast, which was still damp, and then an early dinner came, and finally orderlies piled her unceremoniously on a gurney for a trip to the X-ray room.

Although she'd visited her mother in the hospital, she herself had never been ill and had never been a patient. She had time now to consider all the indignities, and she hated every moment of it. She hated the hospital gowns, the bright smiles of the staff, and the hearty greeting of the X-ray technician. She hated squirming on the cold steel table and feeling so powerless. And she hated feeling so helpless every time she thought of David Farrar. She hated the way he had so completely taken control of her life, and she wondered whether he did that with everyone. No one seemed able to say no to him.

Hours with him. Days with him. The prospect was daunting.

Minutes later she knew exactly how daunting.

He was in her room when she'd returned, and a number of packages sat on a chair at the side of her bed.

She tried to keep her eyes steady as she opened them, but she knew her pleasure must have shown in her eyes. The first box contained a crimson velveteen robe with long, flowing sleeves, and the second two differently designed gowns of a slightly paler shade. There was a pair of slippers in a third box. "I couldn't buy just one slipper," he explained with a chuckle as he looked down at the cast where only her toes protruded.

The clothes were all in impeccable taste, attractive but modest, warm but not bulky. There was also a local newspaper and a bag full of publications rang-ing from news magazines to a West Virginia guide. Guilt struck her as she considered the cost, and she looked for bills in the package, finally looking up at him with frustration.

"It's small payment for my son's life," he said simply.

"My newspaper—" she started.

"The newspaper can do something else. It felt good shopping for a woman again. Don't deprive me of the pleasure."

She looked up at him, and knew his pride would be hurt if she refused. Laney grinned defeatedly and nodded.

His mouth relaxed with the slow smile that made every muscle inside her tighten with reaction. "I think you'll like Cade's Valley."

A now-familiar electricity streaked between them, along with a warm awareness that something special was happening. Warning bells exploded in Laney's head, telling her to move with caution. And by now she knew exactly how to do it. "If you'll give me my story . . ."

"Are you always so persistent?"

"Always."

"I'll tell you about Cade's Valley," he said after a pause, "but you have to make me a promise."

"What?"

"You will wait until you see it all, until you meet the people, before you write anything."

"How long?"

"Ahh . . . such a suspicious voice," he returned with a smile. "I might keep you forever. I have a cellar full of captive reporters." David wondered if he was doing the right thing, but he didn't want the type of story she'd obviously come to write. Perhaps with time he could convince her to do something else, like focus on the need for industry in communities like Cade's Valley.

"Locked up tight?" Laney's voice pierced his thought. "Or do you merely break all their legs?"

It took him a moment to put the remark in context, and then he grinned. "I didn't think about that until now," he teased, a light making his green eyes sparkle. "But perhaps that's an idea."

"An expensive one if you clothe them all."

"Just the pretty ones," he shot back.

"Farrar doesn't sound like an Irish name," she said.

His mouth quirked up in question.

"Blarney, Mr. Farrar. You're full of it."

"David, since we'll be living together."

"Briefly."

"Remember your promise," he stated.

"I haven't made it yet."

"Oh, yes, you did. You didn't say no."

"Neither did I say yes."

"No," he said agreeably, "but you will."

"Do you always get your way?"

The smile fled from his mouth again, and his eyes were unexpectedly desolate.

"No." There was sadness in his voice, and Laney was consumed by the need to reach out and touch him, to chase away the shadows that had appeared so quickly in his eyes. She was shaken by the strength of the emotion, by the power that made her care so deeply. It didn't make sense. She barely knew him. Yet her eyes met his, and they held, each searching for whatever it was that made impossible any movement. Fire and storm touched both of them, reckless and vibrant and full of turbulence.

Down, boy, David told himself. Remember what you pledged to yourself.

Fool, Laney berated herself. Didn't she ever learn?

Yet she could no more tear her eyes from him than she could say no to him.

It's the accident, David thought. She looks so vulnerable.

It's the accident, Laney knew. She was still woozy from the drugs. Otherwise she would resent the way he was taking over her life, making demands he had no right to make.

But he couldn't make his gaze move from the confusion in the dark chocolate of her eyes.

She couldn't stop watching the challenging glare of the most incredible eyes she'd ever seen. She clutched the magazines he'd brought, forcing her gaze down to them with pretended interest.

Laney didn't see them though. She saw in her mind's eye only the gaze she felt still fastened to her. Finally she heard his voice, and she wondered whether it was really unsteady or whether she was.

"You need some rest," he said. "I'll be back later."

She looked up. She didn't want him to go. He didn't want to go; she could tell the way he hesitated, the way he didn't move.

How could this be happening? She hid her confusion with a slight nod and closed her eyes as if to sleep, not wanting to watch him leave.

When she heard the babble of some young voices, she opened her eyes. He was gone, his place taken by several teenagers who had come to see one of the other patients in the room. Then there were more visitors, and she tried to close her eyes, to hide the sudden loneliness that overtook her. A few more days, she told herself, and she would be home. Home in Washington, among her own friends.

But somehow the loneliness didn't go away.

Laney remembered the feel of David Farrar's arms. She had even dreamed about it during the spasmodic bouts of drowsiness and sleep in the past day and a half.

They felt even more secure now as they lifted her from the wheelchair into the back of the Jeep. The motion still seemed effortless to him, although her weight had increased with the cast, which went from above her knee to her foot. She felt as if she weighed a ton.

The most remarkable thing was the gentleness with which he held her, with which he nudged her into the back of the Jeep still piled high with pillows. She smelled the clean, intoxicating aroma of soap and after-shave.

In all her life she'd never felt the protectiveness that David provided so freely. She had taken care of herself longer than she could remember, and she'd always fiercely protected that self-reliance. Until now. She didn't understand the new feelings his nearness gave her, or her surrender to his care, but she couldn't deny the lazy pleasure she experienced in his company, the soft flow of contentment as he carefully pulled a quilt around her.

It was another glittering day, that Sunday. The sleet and rain had disappeared under bright blue skies that were, nonetheless, cold enough to maintain a sheen of ice over much of the landscape. Rays of sunlight glinted against icicles and patches of snow, decorating them with threads of gold.

Hills rose up around them, serving as guardians to the small valley city served by the hospital. Laney felt a rush of delight at the pure raw beauty of the country, a sense of awakening, of being sharply alive and aware. She realized she hadn't felt this energy for months, perhaps not ever.

"Comfortable?"

David's deep voice vibrated in the Jeep. She nodded, and he shut the door and climbed into the front seat. "Did you ever call anyone?"

"Yes," she said as the Jeep started a rumbling of its own. Laney remembered the reference to a dragon and had to smile.

"And . . ." he prompted.

"And everything's fine," she said coldly. She didn't want to tell him that Patrick had immediately offered to provide ambulance service back to Washington and anything else she might need. His voice had been filled with concern and something close to guilt. Patrick knew she had no relatives, and he had partially filled the role during the past several years.

But what she'd so desperately wanted several days ago—to get back to Washington—was suddenly no longer important. It was the story, she kept telling herself, just as she'd told Patrick. She never left a job undone. She'd listened silently to Patrick's protest and then told him flatly she was going to see the story through. He could expect his feature on time.

There had been a pause, a long, quiet, thoughtful break, and surrender. "Do what you think best, Lane, but let me know if there's anything I or the paper can do."

As stunned at her own behavior as he apparently had been, she had agreed quickly before he asked any more questions.

"Have you seen much of West Virginia before?" David said.

"On campaigns . . . but then you really don't have time to see anything."

"Campaigns?"

"I was covering Senator Tribling's campaign," Laney explained.

"You're a political reporter?" There was a trace of puzzlement in his voice.

"Yes." There was both defiance and pride in her voice.

"Then how . . . ?"

Laney winced. Rural teacher or not, he obviously knew the hierarchy of reporters.

"My editor thought it would be a . . . nice change."

He chuckled. "But you didn't?"

How did he know? The pause between her own words? "You would have made a good reporter yourself," she said dryly.

"I thought about it at one time," he said, surprising her by not asking more about why she needed a nice change.

"And?"

"And I decided to teach instead," he said. The words were so carefully said that Laney knew much lay behind them.

"How long have you been teaching in Cade's Valley?" she said, the reporter's instinct now at full bay, her mind memorizing details while she mentally wished for notebook and paper.

"Awhile." There was amusement in his evasive answer. "But I was asking about you."

"There's nothing to tell."

"Except how such a pretty lady came to Cade's Valley."

"An editor's whim," she said.

"Or fate," he said, surprising her.

"Surely you don't believe in fate?" Laney accused him.

"Don't you?" Again his voice was amused, teasing.

"I think people make their own fate."

"No magic or fantasy or fairy godmothers?"

"None of the above."

"Not even at Christmas?"

"Especially not at Christmas."

"I'm harboring a Scrooge? No wonder your editor sent you here. Your journey into the present? Or the past?"

David Farrar was prying into the deepest part of her. But even while Laney knew she should resent the intrusion, she was also aware that she was enjoying the challenge hugely.

"And what role do you play?" she countered. "The nephew? Or Tiny Tim?"

He chuckled. "I'm naively optimistic, you mean."

Laney allowed the silence to speak for her.

"I can see I have some work cut out for me," he said. "I've always loved Christmas."

"Why?"

"Are you scribbling in that mental notebook of yours?"

"If you mean are we on the record, yes."

"Then I refuse to answer on grounds I'm sure you're familiar with."

"Why?"

"Do you always ask so many questions?"

"Of course. Don't you ever answer any?"

"Yours, perhaps. Not the world's."

"Then for now consider the notebook closed." The words surprised even Laney. But her hunger to know more about the enigmatic David Farrar merited a temporary truce.

He shifted slightly in his seat, as if debating with himself. Wearing the same green cable-knit sweater he'd had on two days earlier, he looked ruggedly appealing, as though he would be well at home high on a Irish cliff or at the helm of an old sailing ship.

Fantasy. Magic. And she didn't believe in either.

She suddenly wanted to know why he did.

"Why do you like Christmas?" she asked again.

He mused a moment before responding. "Because, I suppose, it always brings out the best in people. It revives their hopes and dreams, their dreams for a better world, perhaps."

"But doesn't that make it artificial? An excuse not to be their best the rest of the year?"

He coughed. "You *are* a cynic."

"Is that an admission that I'm right?"

"Oh, no, my friend. The holidays, Christian or Jewish or any other religious holiday, merely bring our good qualities, those that lie deep inside, more to the surface, allow us to more openly express feelings we're often embarrassed to show at other times."

"Is that what you're trying to do with your project?"

"Not exactly."

"Then what?"

"You'll have to see for yourself."

"And you will show me? Everything?"

There was a long pause. "There's more than one story in Cade's Valley. Are you willing to look at it all?"

Oh, yes, she thought to herself. Perhaps it would help her understand David Farrar, who was becoming more and more a mystery to her. A beguiling, compelling mystery. "Yes," she said aloud.

"Then you will," he said softly. "I think you will." And the warmth of his voice already made her begin to believe again in fantasy.

Five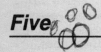

David stole a glance through the rearview mirror at the backseat of the Jeep and wished his passenger was not so damned pretty.

They had ridden in silence for the last few moments, and now her face looked thoughtful, even wistful. The rich brown hair had been brushed to a bright sheen and a dab of color highlighted lips made for kissing. Continuous blasts of physical awareness between them heightened the temperature in the Jeep far more than the heater did.

David couldn't imagine why he was entertaining such thoughts. Just from the conversations they'd held, he'd detected a one-minded dedication to a career. He understood it and sympathized with it, but he also knew that he didn't care to compete with a glamorous and demanding profession.

He had given in once to a woman who'd wanted a life much different from the one he did, and now he was finally doing what he wanted with his life. Exactly what he wanted. If, he added fairly, he didn't count those occasional moments when he longed for adult companionship, for those intimate whispered moments between people who cared for each other.

But usually those thoughts disappeared quickly under the demands of his children and his job. There was always something to do, always a need to fill, whether it was giving a student additional attention or working with the remaining businesses in the community to bring in industry. So far all such attempts had failed, but they continued to go after any lead they could.

His was a rich life, rich in satisfaction, in physical beauty, in watching his sons grow in a community unsoiled by drugs and crime, in a place they didn't have to be watched every moment.

So why did he feel a certain emptiness and need? The much-too-attractive woman in the back of the Jeep made him feel as he hadn't felt in years, like a boy eyeing his first girl. He looked back in the mirror.

"I have three days of school left before the Christmas holidays," he said, seeking to pierce the silent tension in the car. "Mabel has agreed to stay over for the next few days to keep you company."

"Doesn't she have a family?"

"She's a widow, and she's delighted to help."

"I'll pay for it."

His back stiffened. "Don't you ever think of anything but money?" The words came more roughly than he'd intended. But damn, her words reminded him of Julia's obsession with money, and he privately admitted to a touch of wounded pride.

"The newspaper . . ." she started defensively.

"Mabel wants to do it. Theo is like one of her own, and she's grateful. If you offered her money, she'd be insulted."

"But . . ." Laney started to defend herself.

His voice softened. "I'm sorry, I shouldn't have snapped, but Mabel would be hurt if either you or I offered to pay her. We're sort of her adopted family. She doesn't have any children of her own, and staying at the house was her idea." A note of amusement crept into his voice. "I think she feels she has to protect my reputation."

"Humph," Laney replied in a mollified voice. "What about mine?"

"You're an outsider. You don't have one."

"And you do?"

"Absolutely impeccable," he answered in a righteous and wry voice.

"Why do I find that hard to believe?"

"Opportunities are slim."

"I find that even harder to believe."

"Ah, is there a compliment in that statement, Miss Drury?"

"More of a professional observation. And you might as well call me Lane."

"Lane is a male's name," he said dryly. "I was all prepared to give Lane Drury short shrift."

"If there hadn't been an accident, would you have given me the same short shrift?"

There was a long silence, then a chuckle. "Let's say it would have been far more difficult." He hesitated, consumed by the unexpected need to know more about her. She appeared so multifaceted, like a bright jewel that hid its complex center beneath a glittery, even sometimes brittle, surface. "Where did the name come from, or is it something you use for the newspaper?"

"Oh, it's mine all right," she said. "It was the only thing my father ever gave me."

The reply was said lightly, yet there was a bitterness behind it that made his heart clutch. But he didn't say anything, allowing his silence to ask questions he was reluctant to voice.

"My father wanted a boy. When he didn't get his wish, he named me and disappeared."

"I'm sorry," he said. The gentleness in his voice told her that he really was.

"It doesn't matter." Laney almost immediately regretted that moment of revealing so much, yet there was something about the intimacy of the Jeep, the sonorous sound of his voice, the comfort in his words that made her open parts of her soul she'd kept closed since a child.

"Losing a parent always matters."

"You can't lose what you never had."

"And your mother?" he said softly.

"She died just before I graduated from college." The flatly stated answer didn't invite additional questions.

He was silent and for some odd reason she felt the urge to talk about her mother, something she'd never done before. Despite his few words, she could feel his sympathy. No, more than sympathy. Understanding.

"I wanted to give her things she'd never had."

"Things?"

"A comfortable place to live, some nice clothes, some luxuries."

"She had you."

"I just meant bills and more bills."

"I doubt she looked at it that way."

"How could she not?"

"Lane . . . do people really call you Lane?"

"Friends call me Laney."

"I think I like that much better." And he did. It was softer. Gentler, like the look in her eyes when she'd asked about his child right after the accident.

He looked again in the mirror. She had moved slightly, and her face was hidden from his view. But he didn't miss the swell of lovely breasts under the bright red robe.

"Laney," he started again. "I imagine your mother was very proud of you."

"But I could never do anything for her. . . ."

"Just to be is usually enough."

"You don't know—"

"No," he said. "I didn't know your mother. But I know each minute with my sons is something fine."

Laney knew an ache deep inside. She'd never felt that kind of acceptance. She remembered her mother as being tired, always too tired to give her much affection or time. Laney had always felt guilty about that fact, felt responsible for her father leaving her mother.

And again she felt terribly vulnerable, the way she had as a child before she'd taught herself not to care so much that she didn't have a father, that her mother never had time. . . .

Almost desperately she searched for another subject. "How much longer?"

"Before we reach home? Not long. Be prepared. You'll probably be attacked by my boys and their assorted animals."

"The dogs, you mean?"

"And Long John."

"Long John?"

"Our cat."

Laney suddenly chuckled as she remembered the three-legged cat. "Of the Silver family, I presume."

"Right. That was Theo's idea."

"Are there any more?" Laney asked the question almost whimsically, thinking of Henry and Gertrude and Long John.

"There's also Samantha."

"Dare I ask?"

"Our rabbit."

"And . . ."

"Do you really want to know?" All the seriousness was gone now, and his voice was almost lilting with laughter.

"I think I'd better," Laney replied apprehensively.

"Lollipop."

"A cobra?" Laney tried to imagine the most absurd thing she could.

His laughter, deep and rich, echoed through the car. "Don't even suggest it. Theo captured a small black snake once and nearly gave Mabel a stroke. Lollipop is a hamster."

"Dogs and a cat and a rabbit and hamster. All in one house. Don't they go after each other?"

"No, strangely enough, they don't. Sometimes I feel we live on Noah's ark, but we'll keep them out of your way."

She shook her head, then remembered he couldn't see her. "No, I like animals."

David quickly realized she didn't want to talk anymore about herself. He'd been pressing, but then, she fascinated him. So he continued. "Do you have any pets?"

"They don't go together with traveling, or the hours I keep," she said, and there was regret in her voice.

"You'll probably overdose on them during the next few days."

"David?"

He liked the sound of his name on her lips. She had a husky voice, feminine and very sexy. It was particularly so when she spoke slowly, as if thinking about every word before uttering it.

"Uh-huh?"

"I don't know if this is a good idea."

His eyes met hers in the mirror. Even in that indirect way, attraction streaked between them, bold and brash and undeniable.

"Me either," he admitted, and they both knew what the other meant. It wasn't inconvenience; it wasn't pets; it wasn't anything but the raw magnetism between them. "But let's give it a try. It's a long way to Washington."

She wanted to stay. She wanted to learn more about David Farrar and what made him tick. She had never met anyone like him before, and she'd never felt so attracted to anyone. She certainly had never talked to anyone as much, not about things important to her.

She wanted to know why.

But she had no time to consider the question, for the Jeep slowed and they pulled onto the road she'd traveled so disastrously days earlier.

Despite the brightness of the winter sky, the immediate landscape looked bleak. Perhaps, Laney thought, it was the usual winter bareness—skeleton trees without leaves, straw-colored grass, and raw patches of earth. But looking beyond them were the mountains, standing majestic and protective, and they told another tale, a tale of rugged independence. Like David Farrar.

The Jeep came to a stop, and the door of the house flew open, one boy running down the driveway, the other following at a more deliberate pace.

David unwound himself from the seat, stretching long legs before opening the door to the backseat.

"Ready for the melee?" he said, his eyes dancing in the dusky light of the Jeep.

Laney couldn't help but grin, though the ache in her leg was back. The pain pill she'd taken just prior to the ride had obviously run its course. She winced as he picked her up, and she saw his quick worried frown just as the boys reached them.

Laney searched her memory. The older one was Abe. The younger, Theo.

"Gee, it's great having you here," Theo said, bursting with enthusiasm. "A reporter. Awesome."

Abe was more reserved, just as he had been the

first day. He nodded shyly, his bespectacled eyes full of curiosity. Laney remembered herself at that age, how bashful she herself had been until she'd learned to conquer her shyness. "Thank you," she said softly in their direction, "for having me."

Abe grinned suddenly, a replica of his father's warm smile. But it was Theo who answered. "Henry's glad you're here, too."

"I'd like to hear Henry express that," she said with a smile full of companionable mischief. Abe's smile grew wider.

"Me too," David interjected, "as soon as we're inside. Theo, go open the door. Abe, there's some crutches in the Jeep. Bring them inside."

Laney thought his arms must be breaking, yet he showed little strain other than the brief impatience in his voice. There was also a folding wheelchair in the Jeep, but he'd made no effort to take it out and use it, and the thought gave her sudden fierce satisfaction.

It was astounding how much she enjoyed the strength of his arms, and the lean feel of his body. Each time he touched her, the attraction between them accelerated, spurred on by the intimacy of contact, like a locomotive headed down a mountain without brakes. She felt the same trembling fear she might if she were aboard that train.

That fear didn't lessen, even as they entered the house and she became aware of the delicious smells filling it. The living room was much as she remembered it, still littered with packages and papers. There was a roaring fire in a large fireplace she had not noticed before. Henry barked a greeting and was shoved by the smaller but apparently more aggressive Gertrude.

David hesitated just inside the doorway. "The sofa or the bedroom?"

For the past two days Laney had thought that she would love some privacy, but there was a warmth about this room, about the anxious faces around her, that was undeniably compelling. She didn't want to lose it. Not now.

"The sofa," she said.

Once again it had to be cleared, and she looked at David questioningly as he lowered her. Suddenly pillows were behind her, and she was sitting there with three pairs of human eyes and two pairs of dog eyes on her.

The woman she'd seen briefly on Friday entered, and David smiled with obvious affection, the lines around his eyes crinkling. "You remember Mabel?"

Laney reached out a hand, feeling it grasped warmly. "Mightly glad to have you here," the woman said, beaming at her. "Supper's almost ready," she said. "All of Mr. Farrar's favorites."

Laney didn't particularly want to look back at her host. He did too many strange, dizzying things to her, but her eyes inexorably headed his way. His hair was windblown, his face slightly flushed by the cold and exertion. The green sweater deepened the color of his eyes, and he exuded pure masculinity.

She noticed that he had small dimples in his cheeks as he smiled. How had she not noticed that before? Perhaps it was this particular smile that he bestowed on Mabel. It was devastating in its totality, and she realized that the smiles he had given her had been partially guarded.

The thought hurt far worse than it should.

Laney knew suddenly she would do almost anything if that smile were directed to her.

Careful, she told herself. You'll be gone in a few days, back living in a world you understand. She caught herself blinking, and he moved over to her swiftly. "Do you need anything?"

She did. She needed a lot of things at the moment, common sense most of all. But she shook her head.

"Can I get ya a cola?" Theo said, eager to be of help.

"I think that sounds wonderful," Laney replied. Anything to divert her from where her wayward thoughts directed her. She looked around the room, at piles of clothes and toys and boxes. "These are for your students?"

"Yep," David said, and part of the glorious smile slipped from his face.

"Are you wrapping them?"

He shrugged. "They're more special to the kids that way. And Theo and Abe enjoy doing it."

"Dad too," Theo said, reentering the room with a glass in his hand.

"We sort of have a contest," Abe said shyly. "We see who can wrap the most packages."

"And who does?"

Theo looked disgusted. "Abe always wins."

Laney glanced over at Abe, who shrugged just as his father had. It was an incredibly endearing gesture. "It's just that I don't get distracted like Theo."

"Abe," David said fondly, "is our perfectionist. Theo usually decides he would rather decorate the dogs."

"Perhaps I could help," Laney said before she thought about it, thought about getting that involved in someone else's life.

"Gee, would ya?" Theo asked.

"Would *you*." David corrected his son patiently, as if he hadn't done it hundreds of times.

"Oh, Dad, that's what I said," Theo said dejectedly.

David rolled his eyes at Laney, and she couldn't help but grin back. "Any assistance is welcomed," he said easily, "but don't feel that you must."

"I won't," she said.

"There plenty of books in my office," David said. "A little bit of everything. Current novels, history, biographies, mysteries. Just tell me what you like. And Sam—he's our next-door neighbor—fetched your suitcase from the hotel. It's in your room, along with your pocketbook." He stood there, looking awkward for the first time since she'd met him. "I . . . we want you to be as comfortable as possible."

"But it sure would be neat if you helped with the wrapping," Theo persisted.

"Theo!"

Theo looked innocently up at his father. "If she wants to, Dad . . . ?"

"And I do." She looked at Theo's hopeful eyes, and wrapping packages suddenly seemed very appealing. She'd never done much of it. Most of her life, there had been only her mother and herself and, after her mother's death, a few small gifts for friends. She'd never known quite what to buy and had never been very comfortable in doing so, nor in presenting them.

Now there were mountains of gifts, all destined for people who apparently needed almost everything, if her brief ride through the countryside was any indication.

It wasn't as if she had anything else to do.

Except, of course, interview David Farrar, and what better way to do it.

He, however, was looking doubtful, almost as if he were reading her mind.

The thought sent a wave of defensiveness through her. She was the one who usually read thoughts. She was small, slight in build, and her wide eyes, she knew, usually misled people into thinking her young and naive. It was often too late when they discovered otherwise.

But David—strange that she thought of him so easily as David—seemed to know everything she was thinking. It was disconcerting. It was irritating. It was . . . challenging.

So she challenged right back. "Do you object?"

"Of course not," he said easily, but she didn't receive the same smile Mabel had.

From the wry twist of his mouth, she suspected he thought her interest would be short-lived.

"And I'll take you up on your offer of books."

"Good," he said. "I've always thought reading the best sleeping pill there is."

"Or the best keeper-awake."

"That too," he agreed. "After dinner I'll take you for a ride in your limousine, and you can browse to your heart's content."

Laney glanced at the wheelchair in the corner with dislike, but merely nodded.

His eyes caught hers, and held them. They were searching, drilling straight through to all the secret parts within her, and she had to force herself not to try to look away. She didn't want to give him that satisfaction. She didn't want him to know she felt so naked under his gaze. So her eyes met his in open competition.

The room crackled with silent tension. Like a sonic boom, the waves of attraction rocked Laney's world, shattering the protection she had tried to build around her heart.

There might as well have been no one else in the room, no young boys, no animals, no memories. Only the two of them were there, and Laney felt a rush of desire and excitement she'd never felt before. She felt her whole body tighten inside, and her intense need to see him smile at her, to listen to his deep voice, to feel the gentleness of those capable hands, all grew.

Damn.

She was never as glad in her life as when Mabel's voice pierced the fantasy moment, although it took a second for her words to penetrate.

"Supper's ready."

Six

David watched his guest's face. It was a very easy thing to do.

He wondered if she knew how expressive her face was. In the past few minutes it had run the gamut from wariness to challenge to confusion to gratitude at the announcement for dinner.

Or was she merely transparent because he was experiencing corresponding feelings?

Mabel's announcement was as welcome to him as it obviously had been to Laney. David did not care much for his rapidly growing fascination with her. He hoped it stemmed mainly from his recent deprivation of attractive female companionship rather than something more serious.

"Would you like to eat on the sofa or try to sit at the table?"

"Aw, Dad, she wants to eat with us," Theo said.

"Yep," she said.

"Are you sure you're up to it?"

She ignored the ache in her leg that said perhaps not. "I'm sure."

Her eyes had brightened, and David's heart pounded

a little faster. Her decision meant he would have to carry her again. An excuse to hold her again, to feel her arms around his neck.

"I'll be back in a second," he said as he strode quickly to the kitchen and eyed the big round table. He pulled up an extra chair and angled it so Lane Drury could rest her leg. The chair was opposite his usual one.

Mabel winked at him. "She's very pretty."

"Yes," he said shortly, wishing that everyone in Cade's Valley were not steeped in matchmaking. Ever since he came here, every single girl and woman between the ages of seventeen and fifty had, in some fashion, been paraded before him, and he knew he was discussed frequently as an oddity when he showed little interest in remarrying. Residents of Cade's Valley were firm believers in holy matrimony, and David knew he represented a challenge, one the whole community was determined to meet.

So he grimaced at Mabel's latest in a long line of attempts to assist that community endeavor.

"She's going to be here only a few days."

"Plenty of time."

He couldn't help a faint growl. "Plenty of time for what?"

Mabel threw him an innocent look and shrugged. "Just plenty of time, that's all."

David glared at her, but she smiled complacently at him until his mouth bent into a crooked smile of his own.

"You're a hopeless romantic, Mabel."

"Mebbe," she agreed.

"But this time you're wrong."

"Mebbe," she replied with the same knowing smile that was so darned irritating.

David changed the subject, sniffing the various aromas coming up from the stove.

"Fried chicken, gravy and potatoes, green beans, biscuits and honey, and corn," she said. "And pecan pie for desert."

"Mabel, you are a gift from the gods."

"So might be someone else," she said, chuckling. "Those boys need a mama."

"Not her."

"Why not?"

"Because she has her own life and career, that's why."

"Don't mean she can't change. Just like you."

"Ahhh, Mabel . . . I didn't change. I just made a detour."

"Well, mebbe she does too. Anyway, you go git her now before everything gits cold. Pretty little thing." The last was mumbled.

Mabel would find out, David told himself. She would find out at dinner how out of place here Lane Drury was.

Laney took a bite of potatoes with thick milk gravy and looked around the table, wondering at how completely she felt at home. She certainly had not expected to.

She had never been around children much, but these two were a delight, and every time she looked up she found David's eyes on her, their look sometimes cautious, sometimes unexpectedly warm. As she answered the boys' endless questions she quickly discovered how exceptionally bright they were, and she talked to them as she would to any grown-up.

David had started the lively conversation going. "Miss Drury," he announced, "has been covering the presidential campaign."

For a moment Laney had wondered why he'd introduced the subject, but then Abe exploded with questions, his eyes, even behind thick lenses, lighting up like lights on a Christmas tree.

"Who do you think will win?" he asked, his chicken forgotten.

Laney glanced up at David.

"Abe is our political analyst." He grinned. "He can probably tell us more about the campaign than you can."

"Who do you think *should* win?" Laney threw back.

Abe quickly named a candidate and his reasons, all of which were excellent ones. Laney looked at David, one eyebrow raised.

"Abe's our resident genius," he said sheepishly.

"Aw, Dad," Abe said, ducking his head slightly. "You know I'm not any good in math."

"Because you don't try."

Laney noticed there was no censure or acrimony in the exchange, only warm affection and recognition of what must be a recurring argument.

"I wasn't any good at math either," she confided.

"Don't encourage him," David interrupted, but there was a gruff warmth in his voice.

"Dad knows a lot about math," Theo offered. "He was a banker."

Laney lifted her eyebrow. "A banker?"

"In Boston," Theo added happily, obviously pleased to be the center of attention again. His father's lips had tightened slightly.

"In Boston?" Laney echoed, surprise shading her question. How did a Boston banker become a teacher in a small rural school in West Virginia? The question was in her eyes, in her tone of voice.

David ignored it. "More chicken?" There was a slight warning in his voice, and Theo looked at him curiously, then shrugged.

Laney took the offered chicken, though her curiosity was now raging. David Farrar, however, was obviously not ready to supply any information. So for the present she turned her attention to the food.

And then Abe started asking questions, so Laney couldn't pursue her own.

"Have you ever met the President?" Abe asked with wide-eyed fascination.

"Once," she admitted. "Someone took me to a dinner at the White House."

"Awesome." Theo sighed, impressed.

But Abe was beside himself with excitement. "Did you talk to him?"

"For about two seconds," Laney said with a grin. She didn't add that even she, who prided herself on being a blasé reporter, had also thought it a little awesome.

"We went to Washington," Theo informed her enthusiastically.

"And to Congress," Abe added.

"What did you think?" Laney said.

"It wasn't very exciting," Abe admitted. "Only a few people were on the floor and they were all talking to one another. No one was listening to the speaker."

Laney gave him a conspiratorial smile. "Exactly what I thought when I first listened. They do most of their work in committee."

"Will you tell me all about it?"

Laney looked over at David, who rolled his eyes as if she were to embark on a very long, demanding journey, one, she got the impression, he didn't expect her to finish.

Every one of his expressions seemed to be a challenge, she thought, almost as if she had been evaluated and found lacking in some way. She didn't care for the feeling.

She decided to attack. "I would love it," she said to Abe, then turned to look back at David Farrar. "How long have you been in West Virginia?"

"Two years," he said shortly.

"It must be a big change from Boston."

He nodded his head, his eyes suddenly wary again.

"Why?" she added bluntly.

"Why is it a big change?" A light glimmered in those green eyes, and she knew he was delaying, even while teasing.

"Why the move?"

"Why not?"

Another gauntlet thrown.

Frustration must have shown in her eyes, but his lips bent into a small smile. "I like West Virginia," he finally said. "I like the mountains, and the clear streams, and the people."

"But . . . ?"

"But?" he echoed. His tone was short, even impatient, something he had shown little of lately. She knew she should stop. There was time, and it was better to go slowly.

But still, David Farrar having been a banker was such an intriguing thought. The image didn't fit. Just as being a teacher didn't seem to fit. She could see him more readily sitting astride a horse directing a cattle drive, or as captain of a ship, than ruling a classroom. He radiated strong masculine power and self-confidence that defied ordinary labels. And he had no pretensions. David Farrar was a man obviously happy with what and who he was. She wondered if he'd appeared that content in an office.

The urge to know everything about him was overwhelming, and not only because she had a story to do. No one had ever so totally bedeviled her as David Farrar.

He was sitting there, an eyebrow still raised, waiting for an answer to his "but."

She had none to give him. How could she possibly tell him what she was thinking? He would believe she'd had a much harder bang to her head than she had. She was, in fact, beginning to think the same thing.

Laney retreated while retreat was still an option. She shrugged at his question, and turned to Mabel, who had joined them at the table. "That was wonderful. I don't know when I've enjoyed a meal so much."

Mabel beamed, then winked at David before turning back to Laney, her expression changing noticeably into one of worry. "You look real tired, Miss Drury."

Laney grabbed at the excuse. "I am, though the company's been excellent." Her smile included the boys. Theo puffed up with pride while Abe ducked his head slightly.

"I'm sorry," David said. His voice had changed from confrontational to the deep honeyed baritone that was so completely devastating. If she could bottle that sound, she thought, she would be a millionaire.

He pushed his chair back. "I'll take you up to your room."

Once more his arms went around her, one of them awkwardly trying to balance her cast.

Laney put her arms around his neck, her hands feeling the crisp thickness of his hair, and sensation rushed through her. She didn't dare look at his face, so she rested her head against his chest, and she thought she could hear his heart racing. Just as her own was doing.

His body felt so good, so strong, so warm. The scent of soap and spice enveloped her, as did the soft feel of his warm breath against her hair.

He aroused and enticed and teased every one of her senses. Darts of flash fire sped through her body, and she felt herself move closer to the curves of his body.

She closed her eyes, enjoying the myriad sensations, the almost mystic union that was always there when he touched her. Her fingers moved slightly where they touched his neck, and she felt a tremor run through him just as one was running through her.

And then she was sitting down on a bed and looking around, feeling like a small child suddenly deserted by a loved one. She felt weak, so much weaker than she should, and she knew that feeling came from the overwhelming reactions of her body to him. She looked up, and she saw puzzlement on his face.

Although he had put her down, his hand had slipped around hers, and Laney was aware of the magnetic quality of the contact, a coming together that was inevitable.

His other hand moved up to her cheek and touched it, and she felt shivers run through her. When his hand moved slightly to touch a lock of hair, she closed her eyes, not wanting him to see what must be shining there.

"Dad."

The voice shattered whatever magic spell had been woven. The hand moved away quickly, as if burned.

But David's voice was soft when he answered. "What, Abe?"

"Is there anything I can do?"

"Why don't you bring Miss Drury a pitcher of water and a glass," David answered.

"Right," the boy said, and whirled around in the doorway.

Brought back to reality, Laney looked around. She was sitting on a king-size bed in a large masculine-looking room. There were few feminine touches.

The dresser held men's articles—a hairbrush, a plain jewelry box, a framed photo of two boys and a lovely woman. "This is your room," she stated.

He grinned. "Do you always notice everything?"

"It's not very difficult," she said dryly.

He looked around as if for the first time. "All the rooms are like this."

"Perhaps, but this has your essence in it."

David looked amused. "My essence?"

"Don't ask me to explain," she replied ruefully. "I don't think I can."

"Plain and undistinguished, you mean."

"Those are two words I would never apply to you."

"Then which would you?"

She thought. "I don't know yet. But I will."

"Is that a challenge?"

"You've been challenging me all night."

He raised that infernal eyebrow again.

"Don't look innocent, Mr. Farrar."

"I didn't mean to make you feel uncomfortable."

"You didn't," she replied matter-of-factly. "You raised my hackles."

His eyes skimmed over her very carefully, noticing where the robe parted and showed the creamy white of skin. "You hide them very well."

There were all kinds of inferences in his expression, in his eyes. She was trying to sort them out when Abe appeared again, this time with a tray with a pitcher and glass. He showed no signs of leaving, hanging around the doorway instead.

"I don't want to take your room," Laney finally said to David, trying to lighten the sexual awareness that had invaded the space.

"It has a private bathroom," he explained, giving her that particularly wicked crooked grin that was so darn charming. "Don't worry about me. The boys are doubling up, and I'm using one of their rooms."

"But—"

"No buts," he shushed her. "I'll get the wheelchair from downstairs, and a couple of books you might like." He eyed her speculatively. "Mysteries are always good when you're . . . recuperating."

"What about a good Gothic? Set in a small community in an old house during a winter snow-storm . . ."

"With all sorts of small animals . . ."

"And an ominous housekeeper . . ."

"And a brooding master of the house?" David's face assumed a glowering visage, but the twinkling green eyes ruined the effect.

"I think we need some recasting on that part," she said, giggling. "Also on the housekeeper."

David looked offended, but only for a moment. He lowered his brows, and his voice became raspy. "Wait until tonight, my innocent."

Laney's giggle turned into laughter. He looked so endearing, trying to look evil with a face so made for caring.

He started laughing, too, and sat down on the bed. They looked at each other, delighted with their brief nonsense. Laney was laughing so hard, she was almost shaking, and his hand caught hers, his fingers twining with hers as they looked at each other. The laughter flowed, drowning out the tension and brief moment of animosity. They were both doubled over with hilarity as Abe stared at them in wonder before starting to chuckle himself.

Before long, Abe was hunkered down on the floor, laughing. Laney heard the hurried footsteps coming up the stairs, and soon Mabel and Theo had joined Abe in the doorway, both looking on in consternation.

Laney started to explain, but she collapsed into giggles again. A broad smile spread over Mabel's face and she, too, started to laugh.

Theo stamped his foot in frustration. "What's so funny?" he demanded.

That only started new gales of laughter between

David and Laney, and slowly Theo's mouth curved into a smile.

The dogs, summoned by the noise, came up last, followed by Long John. The dogs started barking, and the cat meowed, and every new noise seemed to instigate more waves of laughter.

Finally the laughter was consumed in itself. Tears were rolling down Laney's face, and she saw some at the corners of David's eyes. She looked around at their audience, human and canine, and giggled again.

"I think we've just made a spectacle of ourselves."

"I think you're right, Miss Drury," he agreed, grinning. He was finally giving her *that* smile, and she thought she'd never seen such a wondrous sight. "And I think you need your rest more than ever."

He reluctantly released her hand. "Shoo, everyone," he said, and the onlookers scattered.

"You have them well trained."

"Don't let them fool you," he said. "They probably have another agenda."

"Another agenda?"

"Isn't that what you Washington types say?"

He was teasing her again. Laney wished she didn't enjoy it so much.

"And what do you West Virginia types say?"

"Got somethin' better to do."

She laughed again, although moments earlier she didn't think she had any laughter left. "You're an incorrigible charmer," she said.

"Don't tell my students that."

"They probably already know it."

"Nope," he said. "I work hard at being an ogre."

"Which is why you play Santa Claus," she said, and instantly wished she hadn't.

Some of the light went from his eyes, and the old vigilance crept in. "Is that the reporter asking again?"

"No," she said softly. "Not now."

"Good," he said, but he obviously wasn't going to discuss it further. "I have to get your wheelchair, and see that you're comfortable."

"The doctor mentioned I could use crutches."

"In a week," he said, starting to leave.

"David . . ."

He turned back, his eyes guarded again.

"Thank you for everything."

His wariness melted, and so did she. "Thank *you*," he said. "For my son. And for the laughter."

He walked out of the room, and Laney felt something wonderful shaking the foundation of her being.

Seven

After David returned with the wheelchair and settled Laney in it, he left, and Laney went into the bathroom. There she understood the true meaning of frustration.

She couldn't see herself in the mirror, it was too high. Because of the cast, she couldn't use either the bathtub or shower. She had to satisfy herself with the sink and a washcloth.

Each chore took longer than she thought it should. Her leg continued to throb and, now that she didn't have the distraction of David, her head ached. Her face, she knew, was still swollen. She could feel it.

She wheeled herself out into the bedroom and found Mabel there, along with a stack of books on the night table. "Mr. Farrar brought these for you," Mabel said, "but I think you need sleep more."

Laney yawned. "You're right."

"You're good for Mr. Farrar," Mabel continued. "I've never seen him laugh like that before."

She allowed Mabel to help her into the bed. "Tell me about him."

"When he first came here, he seemed mighty sad,"

Mabel said. He and those boys do better now, but they need a woman's hand. Now, you just go to sleep. You need anything, just call. I'm next door, and Mr. Farrar's down the hall."

The exchange did nothing to speed Laney's sleep, even after she took her prescription. She kept seeing his face, hearing his voice, remembering Mabel's words. . . .

She knew nothing could come of this. Her life was in Washington, D.C. Her life was reporting. Her life was . . . her own. And David Farrar obviously felt as strongly about his.

Or did he? A teacher could teach anyplace, couldn't he?

It was a dumb thought, she knew. Besides, she had vowed never to get involved again. She'd received the impression that David was just as wary for whatever reason.

So why couldn't she blank out those green eyes of his?

Would the impact of those brown eyes never go away?

David tossed in the strange bed. His sleeplessness, he knew, wasn't due entirely to the fact that he wasn't in his own room.

It was partly because Lane Drury was, he admitted to himself.

His hands still felt warm from touching her, his heart beat erratically, and his body ached in a particularly painful way.

He was the one who needed a sleeping pill. He, who'd disdained such things, even at the worst of times. But he had been nearly sleepless for the past three days.

Had it been only three days since he first saw Lane Drury? It seemed longer than that, almost like forever. As if she'd always been someplace in his mind, like a shadow finally revealing itself.

Nonsense, he thought as he turned over for the umpteenth time. They'd simply been together so constantly for the past three days. And she *was* an attractive woman. An attractive woman who would soon be gone.

Forget it, Farrar told himself.

He closed his eyes, willing a sleep that wouldn't come.

When Laney woke the following morning, David and the boys had already left.

He always left early, Mabel had informed Laney when she brought up a magnificent breakfast of country ham, biscuits, and grits. Laney would gladly have forsworn the last item, but she took one look at Mabel's expectant face and found she was unable to disappoint the older woman. She ate, finding that Mabel's version was far superior to what she'd had in the places she'd grabbed her quick breakfasts during the campaign trips.

Since there was no way to get downstairs without David's help, Laney spent the day reading and listening to Mabel. Her luggage included a laptop computer, but she had no enthusiasm for writing. Neither did she have anything to write about. Every time she thought about David Farrar, she realized how little he'd told her.

She tried to milk Mabel, who turned out to be a fountain of information—up to a point.

"Needs a wife," Mabel reiterated. Her eyes were assessing as she said the words.

"Does he . . . is he involved with anyone?" Laney found herself holding her breath.

"That one? No. Not yet. But we have hope."

"Hope?"

"Some real pretty girls around here, and it isn't as if some haven't tried real hard," Mabel said. "When he's through mourning . . ."

"He's still mourning? Didn't she die two years ago?"

"Near 'bout. Came here d'rectly afterward, I reckon. He and the boys were real sad. But they're fine now, fittin' right in. Guess it won't be long 'fore he takes a wife."

The thought was woefully painful to Laney. "He's a good . . . teacher?"

"Isn't anyone more thought of," Mabel said, "though he hasn't been here so long. My cousin's girl says he's the best teacher she's ever had. Sure hope we don't ever lose him."

Laney could practically see the eyes of every girl in the school looking up adoringly. She'd done it herself last night.

"He'll find himself a wife right quick," Mabel was saying. "Right quick." She eyed Laney speculatively. "But I never seen him laugh like he did last night. Sure was good to hear it. Sure was good to see that sparkle in his eyes." And then she changed the subject, asking if Laney felt up to receiving some visitors the following day. "Folks," she said, "wanta thank you for what you did for Theo."

Laney didn't feel she'd done anything for Theo, just what anyone would have done, and she didn't feel particularly up to seeing strangers. But then, perhaps, she thought, she could dig a little deeper into what made David Farrar tick. She nodded.

Moments later, Mabel left, her dark eyes lighting like those of a mischievous crow. Laney tried to read for a while, but her mind kept running over their conversation. What kind of wife would David Farrar choose? What kind had he chosen before? From the picture on his bureau, a very lovely one.

And why did she care?

Hours later, after she'd read the same page at least twenty times without grasping even the slightest meaning, she gave up. The dogs and cat came in, the cat leaping easily to the bed despite the fact he had only three legs. The dogs sniffed her, gently requesting a moment's attention, and Laney found herself grateful for the company. That surprised her. She had always been content on her own before.

Why not now?

Sheila came over, announced that the mother-to-be she'd mentioned the evening of the accident had indeed had her baby. A girl. She quickly checked Laney, proclaimed her in astoundingly good shape though she'd have a black eye for a few days and could expect some lingering pain in her leg. If she needed anything, she should call for her immediately.

"How was the trip?" The question came with a sly look that Laney was becoming familiar with, having spent the morning with Mabel. Laney was fast beginning to understand why David said they needed a chaperone.

"Interesting," she said with impish humor, knowing she would spur speculation.

"How do you like David?"

"Interesting," Laney repeated, enjoying the frustration in Sheila's eyes. The nurse was an attractive woman in her mid-thirties, and Laney wondered whether she had an interest in David herself, until Laney saw a wedding ring. Just that community interest, she guessed. "He's very nice," she amended, and was rewarded with a broad smile.

"Well, got to go," Sheila said. "Remember, if you need anything, or feel poorly . . ."

A late lunch came, and then shadows of winter's early dusk filled the room. She found herself nearly jumping out of her skin with impatience. She wasn't used to being inactive, to being hovered over and lying like a rag doll. But *he* would be home before long, with the boys.

She finally glanced at herself in her mirror compact, and with horror saw a huge black eye that defied every effort of concealment with powder. In disgust, she grabbed her brush and stroked it through her hair two hundred times before she heard the sound of a vehicle turning into the driveway.

Several minutes later there was a light knock on the door and it opened at her ready assent. She'd thought during the day she must have exaggerated his good looks but on seeing him she immediately realized she hadn't. Their effect on her was breathtaking.

He wore a sheepskin jacket, and she felt a stab of delight that he'd not bothered to discard it before coming to see her. His hair was windblown, one undisciplined lock falling over his forehead, his face ruddy with the cold, his eyes a shade deeper than she remembered.

"Hi," he said.

Laney felt tongue-tied. He nearly glowed with life. "Hi, yourself," she replied, feeling like a fool.

His lips twitched. "Not very eloquent, are we?"

"No," she whispered.

David hesitated. "It's strange," he finally said, "but I missed you." It was even stranger, he thought, that he was saying the words. But he'd hardly been able to contain himself all day, and as soon as he arrived home, he'd run up to this room, and the damned words just came out.

Her hands trembled slightly. "I missed you too."

"Not very wise of us, is it?" He'd cocked his head as if considering a problem.

"Not wise at all."

"You look very pretty."

Laney's hand went to her eye.

"Even with that shiner," he said reassuringly. "It . . ."

Laney lifted an eyebrow in challenge. "Go ahead. Try."

"Adds a certain panache?" Laughter twinkled in his eyes.

"A valiant attempt," she said, "but inadequate. Like to try again?"

He grinned. "Oh, we want honesty, do we?"

She chuckled, forgetting her worry under his warm gaze. "No, I really don't think so."

He laughed. "Well, I'll give it to you, Miss Drury. I don't think you could ever look anything but very, very appealing."

Laney felt herself smile. At least he didn't lie and say *beautiful*, but *appealing* would do at the moment. Even if she didn't completely believe him, she felt much better.

"Thank you," she said lightly. "You look in the best of form yourself." She wanted to say more, that he looked downright irresistible, but she couldn't.

His hand seemed to tighten on the doorjamb. "Have you . . . had a good day?"

Laney nodded. "Henry and Gertrude and Long John kept me company. And Mabel's a wonderful cook."

"I know . . . it must be . . . boring for you."

Not boring, she thought. Lonely. Because he hadn't been there.

She shook her head. "Where are the boys?"

"Mabel's feeding them cookies. I told them I would bring you down. Want to go?"

Yes. No. Yes, she wanted him to hold her. No, she wanted to stay here alone with him. The attraction between them was stronger than ever, and it was evident in the stilted tone of their voices, their uncertainty. He'd said he missed her, and then had moved on quickly before either of them could explore the subject any further. But it hung there between them.

She finally nodded. "David?"

He smiled at the sound of his name on her lips. It was soft and beguiling.

He closed the door, and in a few short strides, he was there beside the bed, carefully sitting on its edge. He was so close she could touch him.

She didn't want to, but she couldn't help it. Her hand reached out and rested on his thigh, the touch scorching her even through the material of his slacks. She felt him stiffen, but his hand clasped hers and she felt the chill from the freezing temperature outside. Her fingers tightened, warming his hand, warming her heart.

He leaned down, his lips brushing hers with feather lightness.

Laney closed her eyes, sinking into a sweet quicksand of warm honey. It was both scary and blissful. His mouth was gentle and demanding, hungry and tender, and she felt every nerve respond as they might to tiny electric shocks. Sensations streaked through her body, speeding the flow of her blood, of her breathing.

She felt his arms go around her, pressing her tightly against him, and her hands went up to his neck, encircling it with fingers that played against his skin until she could feel tremors pulse through his body. Her mouth opened under a pressure that was irresistible, and she tasted him as his tongue entered and teased and excited.

Laney moaned, every part of her, every bone, every nerve, every muscle on fire as their mouths explored and savored each other. Their hands also searched and gave pleasure, discovering more mysteries in this vast uncharted territory.

David trailed kisses over her lips, up to the corners of her eyes, with such sweet tenderness she felt her heart quake. Her hand went up to his face and traced the features, resting on the place where she'd seen the dimple. As if he realized her purpose, his mouth broke into a glorious smile. A dimple emerged and Laney looked at it with awe.

David's eyes were cloudy, almost glazed, as he stared back. "This is crazy," David said, his hand trembling.

Her own body was none too steady as she nodded. She couldn't speak, not with the taste and feel of him still so very real.

"I'm sorry." His voice was full of self-condemnation.

"I don't think I am."

His somber expression was lightened by the crooking of one side of his mouth, and the raising of an eyebrow. "Only think?"

Dear God, he was irresistible when he did that. "I *do* do that sometimes—think, I mean." She grinned back, wondering at the great lump forming in her stomach.

"I think you do that quite a lot," he replied quickly, and Laney wondered again at the ease of their communication, even after such heart-stopping moments. Lack of contact with men as a child had made her a little shy around them on a personal basis. It was one reason she'd fallen so hard for Dean. He'd made her feel at ease.

The thought took the smile from her face.

His face also shuttered suddenly, as if in reaction. "Ready to go down?" The tone was businesslike, no longer gently teasing.

"Yes."

He leaned down, and again she felt that raw strength that kept surprising her. She was glad he was able to control his movements, for she was sure she could not. Every bone in her body seemed to turn to jelly when he touched her.

His jacket felt good next to her face; it smelled masculine and leathery and enticing. It was also obviously expensive, like the cable-knit Irish sweater he wore. She wondered how he afforded them on a teacher's salary. Then she recalled that he'd once been a banker. But bankers didn't make much either, unless they were top management.

She lifted her head until she could see his eyes. He was carefully avoiding her gaze as he carried her downstairs, but his arms were steady.

Once again she was settled down on the sofa, still littered with pillows. The fire was going again; the boys were nowhere in sight, and delicious aromas were coming from the kitchen.

"Where are Abe and Theo?"

"Oh, I suppose they'll be here in a minute. They might have taken the dogs for a walk." He hesitated a moment, then asked, "Have you taken any pills today?"

"No."

"Would you like a glass of wine, then?"

"I would love it."

He disappeared into the kitchen and quickly returned with two glasses. "Cherish it," he said. "It comes a long way."

Laney sipped it appreciatively. She didn't drink much, but she knew enough about wine to realize this was a good vintage.

He walked over to an old record player that sat in a corner, and her gaze followed his movements. He stacked several albums, and she waited to see what kind of music would come. She tried to guess, but it was impossible. He was surprising in too many ways.

When soft classical guitar music filled the room, she thought she should have guessed. There was an underlying passion for life in the music, just as there seemed to be in David Farrar, a sense of leashed energy, yet still a softness that wasn't weak.

"I like your choice," she said softly.

He gave her that crooked, appealing grin of his. "I'm hooked on guitar, even play a little, although the boys decry the fact it's not electric. Their taste runs to the noisier."

"I would like to hear you."

"I'm not very good. My repertoire consists of only a few mountain tunes I've picked up. Someday I'd like to put them in a book before they're lost forever."

Laney shook her head. "You continue to amaze me."

"Why?"

"A Boston banker teaching in a small community, and now a folklorist."

He shrugged. "I'd always planned to be a teacher."

"How did you become a banker, then?"

He hesitated. "Between you and me, or the newspaper and me?"

"You and me," she said. She would have promised anything to unravel the mystery. "I promise I won't write anything personal without clearing it with you."

He studied her carefully, as if he were deciding whether or not he could trust her, and Laney held her breath. It was so important to her that he did. Not for any story. That didn't matter anymore. It was desperately important to Lane Drury the woman.

"I was sidetracked when I married," he said. "I fell in love with a banker's only child, and I promised to give her father's bank a try. She'd always had everything. I wanted to keep giving it to her. When I discovered it wasn't working, that I hated banking, she was sick. Cancer. And I couldn't take her away from her family, from the best medical care. So I stayed."

He said the words in a flat, emotionless voice, the kind that hid very deep feelings. She knew, because she used the same type of protection. Pain stabbed deep inside her as she thought of him loving someone so intensely he'd changed the whole direction of his life for her.

"Why West Virginia now?"

"I went to college on a scholarship from the University of West Virginia," he said. "And I did my practice teaching in a community like this."

"And . . ." she urged.

"I like it," he said simply. "I feel I can make a difference. I know that sounds pompous, but . . ." He shrugged.

"Teachers can make a difference anyplace."

"Do you know how difficult it is to get teachers in areas like Cade's Valley?" His voice was harsh.

She shook her head.

"It's practically impossible. Good teachers are at a premium. School systems vie for them. They often offer to pay for trips for interviews, educational assistance, even bonuses. What does Cade's Valley have to offer?"

"It obviously offers you something," she said.

David looked startled at her retort, then grinned crookedly. "Well, I'm eccentric. If you don't believe it, ask my in-laws."

"They disapproved?"

"That's a minor way of putting it. Teaching is a profession for those who can't do anything else, in their opinion. And how can I support my children in a manner to which they'd been accustomed?" His voice was suddenly bitter. "It was a manner I didn't care to continue—living in a condominium, afraid to let them go on the streets to play, substituting things for friends. They couldn't even have pets."

"You seem to have made up for that," she said with amusement.

He chuckled, some of the anger fading from his voice. "And you haven't even met Lollipop yet."

She shook her head.

"And you," he asked suddenly. "How did you happen to become a reporter?"

"Curiosity," she said. "I've always been full of curiosity. Journalism seemed the best way to satisfy that urge in a socially acceptable way."

He leaned back and laughed. "I've already discovered that trait of yours. You remind me of a groundhog who keeps burrowing under whatever obstacle it finds."

"Now, that's a great compliment for a journalist," she said.

"But a bit uncomfortable for the person owning the property. He never knows when he's going to trip and fall into a hole."

Laney's eyes gleamed with appreciation. She'd never felt so alive with a man, so challenged, so completely absorbed in give and take. "I don't think you'd get tripped so easily."

"Unless it's an unusually pretty groundhog."

She almost choked. "I didn't think any groundhogs were particularly glamorous."

"I'm not talking about glamour. . . ."

Whatever else he was going to add was lost in the sound of a door slamming. Theo bounded across the room, with Henry following him in a similarly exuberant manner.

"How d'ya feel, Miss Drury?"

Laney couldn't help but grin back. Theo was the ultimate Huck Finn: straw-colored hair, a brushing of freckles over a turned-up nose, a wide, guileless smile that Laney suspected concealed great reserves of mischief.

"As fine as a groundhog with lots of tender earth."

"Huh?"

Laney glanced up at David's twinkling eyes, and then back down to Theo's confused ones. "I feel very well, thank you," she said formally. "But call me Laney."

"Gee, can I?" Theo looked up at his father.

"Yes, of course, if that's what she prefers."

"Laney," Theo tried. "Would you like to see Lollipop?"

"And Samantha," Laney said as Abe had joined them.

"Right away." Theo beamed and dashed off again, with Abe behind him.

"You made their day," David said. "They love showing off Samantha and Lollipop."

"Where do Samantha and Lollipop live?"

"In the boys' rooms. Just like the dogs. Henry sort of thinks he belongs to Abe, and Gertrude to Theo."

"And Long John . . ."

"Long John rules everyone indiscriminately."

Laney leaned back comfortably and took another sip of wine. The fire crackled behind her; the music was both lulling and demanding with its steady beat. She'd never felt so content, so at home in her life. Warmth was everywhere, especially inside her, her heart swelling with a sense of belonging. She looked up and saw David's crooked smile. Magic. Enchantment. David had mentioned both on the ride from the hospital. And she'd said she didn't believe in either.

But she was beginning to.

Eight

David couldn't take his eyes away from her.

He'd been attracted to Lane Drury from the moment he'd seen her in the wrecked car. That fascination had grown during those few moments of vulnerability at the hospital, but now, as her eyes sparkled and her mouth smiled with true wonder, he thought he'd never seen anyone quite as lovely.

Not even Julia, who'd been a true beauty.

The thought of Julia sent familiar waves of sadness through him. He felt disloyal in comparing the two women; and traitorous for criticizing the life they'd had. But he'd felt so trapped then, so torn between what was best for Julia, for the children, for himself. And then he'd no longer had a choice because Julia came first, Julia and her long battle.

But now he felt good—about himself, his work, the small things he was accomplishing. He'd felt so much satisfaction, he hadn't realized how much he missed other things, like a woman smiling at him, like the excitement that leapt and darted between a man and woman, like the verbal battles that stimulated and challenged.

He felt alive again, pulsing with energy. Every nerve end jerked with sensations he hadn't known in years, and he felt a deep aching heat in his loins.

The warmth in the room wasn't due entirely to the old heater or the fireplace. Neither was the crackle confined to the blaze. Nor the quickening of his blood to the now more throbbing sound of the flamenco music coming from the record player.

He knew these feelings were dangerous. He couldn't get involved again with a woman like Lane Drury, who, like Julia, would never be satisfied with what he could offer.

Abstinence, he told himself. His reactions to her came from nothing more than his self-imposed celibacy of the past two years. He refused to let it be anything else than that. But still, he had laughed more in the past eighteen hours than he'd laughed in months, and it felt good. So damned good.

Lane Drury was looking almost as dazed as he felt, and for a moment silence hung between them, the record having run its course. Yet there was still pulsating tension in the air.

David was grateful when Theo and Abe returned, both carrying small furry creatures. Theo plopped Lollipop in Laney's lap while Abe sat next to her on the floor, cuddling the rabbit.

Lane's face creased into softness as she took the hamster, her fingers gently petting the tiny animal.

"He bites," David warned.

"Aw, Dad, no, he doesn't. Just that one time. He was mad at you."

Laney smiled impishly. "Now, what did your father do to make Lollipop mad?"

Theo looked at his father, then at Laney. "He yelled at me."

"Tell her why," David demanded, feeling his face flush.

"Do I have to?"

"You opened the subject. I didn't," David replied with a small grin that held no reprieve.

"I put a frog in the flour bin," Theo said.

"And nearly scared Mabel to death," David added.

"She wasn't scared. She just pretended like she was."

"Nonetheless, I think Laney should know that she might likely find a frog or snake or even Lollipop in her bed."

Laney laughed. "I used to wish I had a brother who would do that occasionally."

David tried hard to frown but couldn't. "Watch out, Laney, or you might discover the truth about being very careful about what you wish for. You might just get it."

Abe looked up. "You don't have any brothers or sisters?"

"No," she said.

"Or children?"

Laney shook her head.

Abe's solemn eyes seemed to cloud with concern. "A dad?" He couldn't mention *mother*, and David felt pain rush through him. Neither of his sons mentioned their mother.

Some of the laughter went from Laney's eyes, and he remembered their conversation in the car, the bitterness in her voice when she'd mentioned her father.

"Abe, don't ask so many questions," he said in a sharper voice than he'd intended. His elder son looked hurt, and regret instantly filled David. Especially since Julia's illness, Abe's feelings were easily bruised.

"It's all right," Laney said softly. "Remember, I like to ask questions myself. It's the only way to learn." She gave the hamster back to Theo and reached out to touch the rabbit in Abe's lap. "No, Abe," she said, "I don't have a father, and my mother died years ago."

A mist seemed to form on Abe's glasses. "My mother died too."

"I know," Laney said in a gentle tone that surprised David and made him ache inside.

"You can have us as a family," Abe blurted out, and surprise shook David. Abe usually didn't take up with strangers easily, and though David had changed much of his thinking about Lane Drury, there was still a distance about her that would ordinarily put Abe off. But both of his boys had taken to Lane with unexpected swiftness.

Just as he had, despite his many reservations, he thought. There was something very appealing about Lane despite the surface brittleness he had seen in the beginning. He'd loved her unrestrained laughter the previous night, and he was entranced by the kindness in her eyes as she spoke to Abe, and the softness of her fingers as she touched Lollipop and Samantha.

His breath caught in his throat as she regarded Abe with a tenderness that couldn't be feigned. "I'd like that very much."

Mabel appeared then, announcing dinner, and the moment was gone as the boys rushed to take their pets upstairs and wash their hands. David brought Laney a wet towel to wash her own, before lifting her once more and carrying her to the table.

He wished he didn't quake and almost stumble, not from the weight, for she was light even with the cast, but from the exhilaration of touching her, of feeling her skin against his, of sensing her complete trust. It had been a long time since he'd felt a woman's trust.

When she was seated, she looked up at him, her eyes wide and wondering . . . and unbelievably captivating. They were so deep and swimming with so many emotions that he wanted to explore. Slowly. Intimately.

And then he remembered there was no time. She would soon be gone from his life, and that of his children, as suddenly as she had come into it.

He steeled himself and his feelings against her.

But steeling did damned little good, he discovered as the evening went on.

He was silent during dinner, letting the boys dominate the conversation with question after question. Laney Drury answered them all patiently, often with unexpected humor that took a moment to soak in, and then delighted grins broke out among her listeners.

After dinner there was package-wrapping. David explained to Laney that his students knew gifts had been donated by corporations, and some would be handed out at a special party at the school on the last day before Christmas vacation. The remainder would be taken to homes late on Christmas Eve so the parents could give them as they wished—as presents from the parents themselves or Santa Claus or as if they'd appeared by magic.

David liked the quick ray of understanding in Laney's eyes, and her obviously sincere offer to help wrap packages. So many items had flooded in from various corporations and businesses that there were enough for each of the one hundred eight children in the whole school, not just the thirty in David's seventh, eighth, and ninth grades. There were even items suitable for preschool children in the community.

After David had deposited Laney back on the sofa, he showed her the lists. There were lists and lists. One four-page list included clothes sizes for each child. Another included suitable toys for each. There were checks next to those that had been wrapped, which included about three-quarters of the items.

Laney raised her eyebrows. "You did all these?"

He shrugged his shoulders as he grimaced wryly. "Sam and Sarah Talley have been coming over and helping, sometimes Sheila, if she's not too busy. Mabel. Some others."

"And Christmas Eve?"

"I play Santa Claus."

"Where do you put everything?"

"The wrapped packages are in a storeroom outside. Most of the unwrapped items are on the screened porch." He nodded to a door she'd not seen open before.

"Tell me what to do," Laney said, infected with David's and his boys' enthusiasm.

Before long Laney was immersed in paper and ribbons and gift tags. She was amazed at the array of donated items. David had written one hundred corporations, and the letter must have been uncommonly effective since most of them responded with donations. In fact, David explained, much more came than they could possibly use, sometimes in full truckloads. What David didn't think he could use was either donated to another community or to the local cooperative, which would then sell the items at low cost. The proceeds would purchase food.

Abe approached Laney with a large box. "Will you help me?" he said.

"What can I do?"

Abe opened the box and pulled out some small-size coats. "I'll read the size," he said, "and you can check the list and see who needs one. Then we wrap it."

David replaced the guitar music with Christmas carols, and before long all of them were humming along, even Mabel, who had appeared to help.

The living room was once more a mess, dogs trampling through paper; the cat sitting haughtily on the old television as he gazed disdainfully at the wreckage before him. Laney looked around and thought nothing in her life had ever been so like a Norman Rockwell painting. In the past she had scorned such scenes, but now . . .

She looked up from the boy's coat she was wrapping and her eyes rested on David. His hands, strong and sure, were also busy, making every crease of paper as perfect as possible, his long fingers tying nearly perfect bows. Her own efforts were not as competent, and she knew a slight frown was forming on her face.

His gaze found hers just then, and warmth darted out to her, as his voice, a pleasing baritone, completed the last few strains of "God Bless Ye Merry Gentlemen." He grinned crookedly at her, almost apologetically at the sentimentality.

She felt soft and melting all over, and she wanted to feel neither. She had her career, which was all she'd ever wanted. She had a top salary, prestige, respect, and a lovely apartment, even if she never had time to use it. She had independence. She would never have to rely on anyone, as her mother had.

She had everything. A few more days and she would be back in her own world. She tried to feel very glad about that.

"Laney, would you help me tie this bow?" Abe's anxious face looked up at her. Laney obligingly put her finger where he indicated, and allowed the bright red ribbon to wrap around her finger as Abe's vulnerable look wrapped around her heart.

Theo was sitting on the floor next to his father, wrapping his own packages rather slapdashedly while Gertrude sat contentedly in his lap formed by crossed legs. He enthusiastically sang "We Three

Kings." His voice was perfectly pitched, so sweet that tears formed in the back of Laney's eyes.

When he'd finished, he looked up at Laney with a big grin. "I'm singing at the school party. So is Abe. Will you come and watch?"

"When is it?" Laney said.

"Wednesday," Theo said. "Will ya? I have a solo all of my own."

"I bet you do," Laney said. "You have a wonderful voice."

Theo's face went red, and he ducked his head slightly at the compliment. "Will ya?"

David was looking away, his face expressionless, and Laney sensed he was waiting for her answer.

Laney wanted to say yes, but she was beginning to learn that every moment spent in this house was dangerous. They were making her discontented in a way she'd never been before, not even in the past few months. It scared her how much she wanted to stay.

"Please come," Abe added. His face suddenly brightened. "And you can help us pick out our Christmas tree Thursday, and that's most fun of all."

Laney looked back at David. His eyes were fixed on the blank television set over which the cat's tail swished.

"Please," Theo chimed in, longing in his voice. Laney suddenly realized how much the boys must miss their mother, and she knew a jealousy of the dead woman.

David's face finally turned back to her, his eyes enigmatic. "The doctor said you should stay off that leg at least a week."

The response was somewhat less enthusiastic than his sons', and she noticed how tense he suddenly was. His hands had stilled.

They had never discussed how long she would stay. At the hospital Laney had thought that she would make her escape as soon as possible, as soon as she got her story. The prospect of being in a stranger's home, completely depending on others for her slightest needs, had not been particularly pleasing. She'd agreed in a drug-fogged moment. But now she didn't want to leave. It shocked her how much she didn't want to leave.

"Will ya?" Theo persisted.

Laney wished she had a better idea of how David felt. Would she even be welcomed? Since their kiss earlier that afternoon, David had seemed distant, wary. Did he believe it a mistake? An aberration?

He remained silent, and she could only guess at his thoughts.

"Perhaps through Thursday," she said as noncommittally as she could.

"You'll come with us to find a Christmas tree?"

Theo's face looked so expectant, so hopeful, Laney's resolve melted. Perhaps, she justified to herself, Christmas-tree hunting could help her story.

The story!

She had gotten absolutely no place with it. She had been so distracted by David Farrar that she'd given little thought to the assignment that brought her there. Her mind tried to sort out what little it had absorbed in the past several hours, and she realized she was feeling much too close to the story.

Bad move, Lane, she told herself. She'd always remained distant from any story, to keep things in perspective. But now, sitting in a firelit room, being pleaded with by two boys and feeling a terrible tingling sensation from the mere presence of a man sitting four feet away, she felt anything but objective and uninvolved.

Her eyes met David's, and she saw the sudden flare in them, the beginning of that crooked, wry smile that did such disastrous things to her usually practical nature.

"I'll tell you what," he said. "We'll go find the tree Thursday, and I'll drive you to Charleston Friday for a plane."

Four more days. Four more days with him.

It was incredibly stupid, but Laney found herself nodding her head. "Where do you go for a tree?"

He grinned. "The woods. One of the advantages of country living. Free Christmas trees."

"But . . ." Laney looked down at her leg.

"Don't worry about that. The Pink Lady can go almost anyplace, through the woods and over the hills."

"The truck outside," she guessed.

"Right."

She felt herself start to giggle. David and a pink truck. Never had she seen such a least likely twosome.

"Don't laugh," he said. "She'd quite handy."

"How did you come by her?"

"She came with the house," he said complacently.

"We liked her lots better than the car we had," Theo said.

David shrugged under the question in Laney's eyes. "Our other car was . . . out of place here, and I sort of liked the old girl."

"Lots of character?" Laney suggested.

"That's one way of putting it," he agreed. "But it is a lot more practical. There are a lot of dirt roads around here."

"What did you do with your other one?"

There was a moment of silence. "He gave it to the cooperative," Mabel said.

David had mentioned the cooperative before and Laney wanted to know more. "Cooperative?"

David shrugged. "They need it to drive people to the doctor or hospital or store."

Mabel gave him a sly look. "Mr. Farrar helped start it."

"The cooperative?"

Mabel nodded.

So much for being a plain schoolteacher, Laney thought. If David was anything, he was neither ordinary nor plain. And he wasn't going to tell her anything. She'd have to find out from Mabel.

"What else has Mr. Farrar done?" she asked, feeling a moment of guilt.

Mabel ignored David's warning frown. "Started a campaign to get some industry or recreation here," she said. "Would mean a lot of jobs."

"And . . ."

Mabel started to open her mouth, but David interrupted. "I think we would all like a cup of cocoa, Mabel."

Mabel tried to speak.

"Mabel." The word was all the order needed. Mabel looked speculatively at Laney before disappearing into the kitchen.

David slowly unwound his long legs, stretching them out in a gesture that dismissed all previous conversation. "I'll go help her," he said, and Laney had the feeling that her one source of information might dry up.

Laney watched David disappear into the kitchen, all lanky strength and grace. Power. That described him. Quiet, effective power. And again she wondered about his past, and what brought him here.

Abe pulled out another coat and gave Laney the size. As she scanned the list she found a matching recipient, and Abe grinned. "He's the one who gave me Samantha."

Laney found another sheet of paper and started wrapping. "How do you like it here, Abe?"

Abe handed her some tape. "I like it fine now. I didn't at first."

"Why didn't you like it at first?"

He blinked up at her. "I missed my school."

"And now?" Laney asked.

"I have Henry and Samantha and Gertrude, and we go for camping trips. I like that. But I miss . . . some things about Boston."

Like his mother. He didn't say so, but the message was in his eyes.

She wanted to ask him more about her, but that would be too much of an intrusion, and she knew instinctively how much David would hate that.

"It *is* pretty here," she said.

"I really like it," Theo said, obviously claiming his share of the attention. "Camping's awesome. Dad plays the guitar, and we sing, and he tells us all kinds of neat stuff."

"Like what?"

"Like ghost stories."

Laney tried to imagine the scene. Two boys hanging on to every word in a small, intimate circle around a dancing fire. She'd never gone camping, but she'd always thought it would be great fun. She'd always been too busy.

"Does he tell good ghost stories?"

"The scariest," Theo replied with a smile.

"And you like scary stories."

Theo shivered with make-believe fear. "Yeah, but Henry's there to scare away ghosts."

"Henry goes too?"

"Of course." Theo looked at her incredulously.

"And Gertrude?"

"Mabel takes care of Gertrude and Long John and the others," Abe replied. "Gertrude might get lost."

"I think camping sounds wonderful," Laney said.

"Mebbe you can go with us sometime," Theo said hopefully.

Abe cast a superior glance at his brother. "She can't," he said. "She won't be here."

Desolation fell over Laney, and she wondered why camping seemed so much more appealing than living in her Washington apartment.

But it did.

A knock came at the door, and David welcomed the couple Laney remembered from the day of the accident. Laney greeted the Talleys warmly, recalling their help, but she couldn't stifle her surprise when they presented her with a small wrapped gift.

"Thank you," she said, but her eyes asked a question.

"Because you helped Theo," Sarah said. "He's real special to us, just like his daddy."

Laney had never felt more of a fraud as she unwrapped the package. She had done nothing special, when it seemed these people had all done so much, particularly David.

She couldn't stop an exclamation of delight, however, as she opened the box and saw a small cross made of stained glass. It was exquisite in design, and obviously made with love and care.

David went over to look at it. "Sarah made it herself. She sells them in Charleston."

Laney looked at Sarah. "It's truly beautiful. Thank you."

Sarah flushed with pleasure. "You're welcome."

David noticed Laney's discomfort. "We're making some cocoa," he proclaimed, changing the subject. Soon they were all sipping chocolate while Sarah asked about the hospital stay.

And then they all plunged back into wrapping, conversation ebbing and flowing, mostly concerning the youngsters for whom the gifts were intended. A doll for Elsie, a cooking set for her sister. A board game for Ray, and a baseball and glove for his athletic brother. Great care was taken to select the right gifts for the right child. Names swam in Laney's head as the children and their needs became real to her.

Her hands grew more accustomed to the activity, hurrying as did the others, because now they had real purpose. She could almost see the faces, imagine their expressions on Christmas.

The time went quickly. It seemed like only minutes had passed when the Talleys excused themselves, and the boys were sent to bed.

Mabel and David shared the cleaning-up duties, while Laney watched, wishing she could participate in the companionable chores.

But it was enough to watch David as he put paper and packages in order and stacked the wrapped gifts with such care. He avoided looking at her, but every once in a while their eyes met, and sparks lit the room with fiery impact.

Laney felt her body tense as the last few items were tucked away. Already tingling with anticipation, she would soon feel his arms again.

And his lips? Would she also taste them again?

And if she did? How could she bear it, knowing she would soon be gone?

Nine

David fought his own demons as he reached down for her and thought about holding her again.

He'd never wanted to kiss anyone so badly before.

He remembered the taste of her, and he craved it.

Even her incessant curiosity was appealing.

But he wanted to keep his life as it was.

Still, as he carried her upstairs, he knew their attraction to each other was growing. He liked her humor, her reaction to others, her rapport with his sons.

Most of all, he liked her response to him. Her eyes livened every time they turned his way, like a brewing storm. And her body seemed to meld into his when he held her.

Watch out, he told himself. You changed your life for a woman once. Never again.

He tried to discipline himself, tried to keep an emotional distance despite the physical proximity.

Once in the bedroom, he placed her in the wheelchair beside the bed. He straightened and looked at her to say good night.

Her cheeks were flushed from the fire downstairs,

her dark eyes were bright and dancing with life, her lips trembling with a tentative smile. The red robe had fallen open around her neck, revealing ivory skin. Her hair, so dark and silky, fell like a cloud around the delicate features of her face.

He was lost.

He reached out a finger and touched her cheek, tracing the fine cheekbones, the curve of her mouth. Gently, it moved up toward her searching eyes, and he wanted to take her back in his arms. Lord, he needed her. He felt his whole body tighten with the agony of wanting her.

David forced his hand away, and he sat down on the bed, hands falling between his knees to keep from reaching for her.

His eyes held so much grief that Laney knew he was remembering painful times, and was associating them with her.

"What is it, David?" she asked quietly.

"What do you want, Lane Drury?"

"Want?"

"Want," he repeated. "Tomorrow? Next week? Next year?"

Her impulse was to say "you." But she knew that life wasn't that simple. She had planned and plotted her future carefully for more than fifteen years. She had followed each step with determination. She had nearly reached the pinnacle of her dream. Dean Kelly had been only a slight detour on the path, one that she'd told herself she would avoid again.

She had wanted success and independence. She'd wanted never to be dependent on a man, for that weakness had destroyed her mother.

But suddenly that didn't seem so important. Or was this all only a momentary aberration, a fantasy that wouldn't, couldn't, last? As Dean hadn't lasted?

"I can answer for tomorrow," she said finally. "I don't know if I can beyond that."

"Then tomorrow?"

"To go to your school with you."

"Why?" The question was harsh.

Because I don't want to spend the day without you. "It would help my story," she said instead.

The damned story. David realized he had been holding his breath, that he'd wanted her to say she wanted to be with him.

"Are you up to it?" he said carefully.

She nodded.

"It will be a long day."

"That doesn't matter."

He searched her face for a few moments. "Perhaps you could speak to my class. About reporting."

She nodded again. She didn't feel comfortable about speaking, had declined to be on the newspaper's speakers' bureau, but she had asked him for a favor and she could hardly refuse his. It seemed a fair enough price for learning more about David Farrar, for being with him.

"I'll be leaving at seven," he warned.

"Are you accusing me of being lazy?"

"You should be lazy," he said. "You have every right to be lazy."

"When we're on a campaign," she said, "we usually get up at five or six, sometimes four in the morning. Seven is a luxury."

"Do you miss it?"

"The campaign?"

He shrugged carelessly although there was nothing careless about the look in his eyes. It was intense. "The campaign, politics, Washington."

She knew the answer; she'd thought about it before. There had been so much excitement and stimulation in the beginning, in spending hours with fellow reporters analyzing this politician and that one, how well each would do in their races. But somewhere along the way the excitement had run its course. Perhaps because familiarity breeds contempt.

Did she miss it now? No. Would she next week? She didn't know. She knew only that it was the one thing she was competent at. Or had been, according to Patrick.

"Yes," she said defensively, a bit of bravado in her voice.

"And this story, the one you were sent here to do?"

"The one you keep avoiding."

He grinned suddenly. "Yeah, that one."

"What about it?"

"Have you decided how you're going to do it?" His voice was suddenly tense.

She shook her head sadly. "My main source won't talk to me."

"Can I interest you in another story?"

"What kind?"

"About communities like Cade's Valley that are all over the South, the Midwest, the Southwest. Once-cohesive communities with strong histories and loyalties and traditions. How they survive despite governmental indifference. Or die." There was deep passion in his voice.

"What's going to happen to Cade's Valley?" she asked quietly.

"The young people move away. Join the army mostly. There are no jobs here, no opportunities, and the poor get poorer. Unless we get some industry or some help with tourism, Cade's Valley will be little more than a ghost town in a few years."

"You really love it here, don't you?"

"I like the people. I like their independence and their stubbornness." He shrugged slightly, as if embarrassed. "And I like the hills, the mountains. There's a wonderful history here, from the Revolution through the Civil War, when West Virginia pulled away from Virginia."

"Independence again," she said, thinking he himself was the epitome of independence. David Farrar was always going to do what he thought right, damn the consequences. She searched her mind, and she couldn't remember anyone like him, anyone who had the iron integrity that was so much a part of him. She also recalled his earlier words, when he talked so briefly about his wife and being "detoured." She sensed he would never be detoured again.

"Independence and a deep appreciation of the land," he added.

"And you help them keep that?"

David frowned, the lines around his eyes deepening as if he questioned the intent of her question. "They don't need help that way. They don't need charity. They simply need opportunity. And then, by God, they run with it."

"But you're obviously helping—the cooperative, the corporation gifts . . ."

His voice was suddenly curt. "A little, perhaps. I'm not egotistical enough to think I can change a lot."

"The bank you worked for—couldn't you use your connections there?"

The light faded from his eyes. "No. Our bank catered to the wealthy. We specialized in making loans to people who didn't need them."

Laney didn't miss the words "our bank." But there was a warning in his voice, and she didn't want to destroy the rapport that was so strong between them. She tried another tack.

"Where are you from?" She'd been trying to determine that since she'd met him.

"A little mining town in Pennsylvania."

"Like this one."

"A little."

"Why didn't you go back there?"

"Too many memories."

"But you're going back in your own way, aren't you?" she said. "You chose a town just like the one you came from."

"A little, maybe. The school was even smaller than this one. One of those one-room schools you hear about, but I had a terrific teacher. She kept me from quitting, and wrote someone she knew about getting me a scholarship."

"Your family?"

"My dad died when I was boy. Black-lung disease. My mother died a year later of pneumonia. My sister and her husband raised me."

"Are they still there?"

He nodded. "They have a farm. It's small, but it supports them. And they're happy. That's what counts."

"You were happy there?"

"Yep," he said. "You would like my sister. She has six children, from six to twenty-two, and she's indefatigable."

They were talking like two old friends, each probing gently into the other's life. Somehow her hand had wandered over to his knee and was resting there, absorbing his warmth. His hand moved and touched it, his fingers caressing hers with light strokes.

There was an intimacy about the touch, a closeness Laney had never felt with anyone before. A sound, almost like a purr, came from her throat as her hand explored the rough strength of his fingers. Nothing in the world existed for her except his green eyes, the mouth set in a small frown, the feel of his skin against hers, the magnetic pull of their bodies as they leaned toward each other.

He reached for her and pulled her gently on the bed, resting her body next to his, her head leaning on his chest. His hands ran up and down her arms as if he couldn't relinquish contact.

She absorbed every touch, lost in the magic of sensations that played between them. His lips touched her hair, his hands moving to her neck and playing along its nape sending shivers of reaction along the length of her body.

Laney tilted her head up until her eyes met his, and his lips moved toward hers, meeting in a soft wonder that quickly turned hungry.

Fire flamed in every part of her body, the heated core centering in her most sensitive nucleus and spreading steadily through her marrow and into her soul. Nothing had ever touched her there before, she realized as everything in her reached toward him in silent desperation.

She had never needed anyone in this way before. So hungrily. So completely. Her hand climbed up, trembling as it came to his face, a face that had become engraved in her heart, a face with troubled lines and strength, with humor and self-mockery, a face that believed in magic while knowing tragedy.

She loved that face.

The sudden knowledge was devastating. Her fingers faltered and hesitated, and her gaze met his, seeing the same shocked realization.

He groaned and moved slightly, but the movement only made their bodies more aware of each other. She could feel the hardness under her and cried inside for it.

She wanted to lose herself in his world. But a lifetime of discipline, of plans to achieve her own dreams, of her fears of losing an identity she worked so hard to build screamed silently in her head.

Laney moved, forcing her body to break the bond with his.

David's face creased into a wry look. "I'm doing it again. I can't seem to keep away from you, lady."

"I'm not doing so well myself," Laney admitted ruefully.

His mouth relaxed slightly. "I never thought mutuality could be a problem."

"Is it?"

He searched her face carefully. "Could you ever be happy in a place like Cade's Valley?"

When he looked at her like that, the answer was yes. But for how long? "I don't know," she said honestly.

"It wasn't enough for my wife either," David said slowly, moving away from her, unwinding his long frame and standing up. Sadness was etched in his face. Regret. Grief. Determination.

"I'd better let you get some sleep," he added after a moment, his voice empty.

Laney felt a well of emptiness herself, as if she'd just lost everything that was important. "Can I still go with you tomorrow?"

"Of course," he said.

"David."

"Yes?" he said, turning back after having started for the door.

"This evening was . . . very . . . nice."

"Thank you for helping." His voice was stilted, forced, and Laney felt pain deep inside. It had been so warm earlier, so full of easy laughter.

"I don't know when I've enjoyed anything so much."

His face remained expressionless, but there was a doubt in his eyes that made Laney's pain deeper.

"Good night," she said finally, unable to bear his scrutiny any longer.

"Good night."

The sound of the door closing was very soft, but to Laney it was like an iron door clanging shut.

David shaved quickly. He had slept little during the night. His body had ached too much, and his mind had been too busy trying to sort out the clutter there.

Julia was there with him. And Lane. Why was he always attracted to ambitious women?

They were different though. Julia had been ambitious for him. His success was also her success. Lane was ambitious for herself. How could he ask her to deny her dreams when he couldn't deny his own?

He didn't blame Lane. In fact, he admired her.

But their dreams obviously didn't match, like oil and water.

He had tried to mix them before. He wasn't going to do it again. It had hurt too damned much.

His in-laws, he knew, thought him mad. When Julia had died, he had inherited one-eighth of the stock in her family's bank, and he had saved money from his own salary at the bank. He could have done nearly anything he wanted.

But he hadn't wanted the money. It had been a trap from the very beginning, and he wanted the money even less when it came from his wife's death. David couldn't help but think of it as blood money.

He'd put the inheritance in trust funds for the boys. He bought this house with his own savings, and put the rest into certificates of deposit, which supplemented his salary.

He had been happy, and he believed the boys were happy here. It had taken time, but now they enjoyed tramping through the woods and watching a sunset with him. They had discovered the fun of sharing. They had grown so much in the past two years, not just in size, but values. In Boston they had merely to mention an item, and it had been given them by their mother or grandparents. Their lives, David often felt, had been measured solely by possessions.

Few things had given him as much pleasure as watching them help plan gifts for each of their friends and acquaintances, to use their time to make others happy.

But their almost immediate response to Laney had been unexpected . . . and even a bit frightening. He had obviously not realized how much they missed having a mother, although he knew they often grieved for Julia.

He couldn't allow them to get attached to Lane, just as he couldn't allow himself to get involved again. Another mistake, another loss, would be too devastating for them all.

He knocked on her door and his voice was curt as he called her name.

He had hoped that she had changed her mind about accompanying him to school. Her presence for ten straight hours would be distracting.

She was sitting on the bed, her long hair neatly done in a French braid, and wearing a practical but very fetching electric-blue blouse and matching gathered skirt. "My one traveling dress," she said a little shyly.

His breath caught in his throat. The color made her eyes larger and darker and more mysterious, and the braid highlighted the fine structure of her face. She looked enchanting and irresistible.

"I think one is all you need," he finally managed.

"It doesn't wrinkle," Laney said.

He could already feel his body react to her mere presence, to the small tentative smile that was so endearing. After the previous night, she must have felt as completely confused as he did.

Already the air was sizzling between them, despite

his repeated warnings to himself against his fascination with her.

Her hand was digging into the bed, just as his own was doing in his pocket, searching for anything to hang on to rather than reach out to her and touch and touch and touch.

"It's been a long time since I've gone to school," she said, her voice trembling slightly in a way that made her seem even more vulnerable, that made his heart more vulnerable.

Dear God, he didn't want to go to school. He wanted to sit down next to her on the bed, and caress and explore and . . .

An identical longing burned intensely in her eyes, making their deep brown color dance with golden fires.

"Don't expect much," he replied shortly, knowing he sounded hoarse.

But her face was ablaze with expectation. The world-weariness that had shown itself several times in the past few days was gone, and Lane Drury looked young and fresh and eager. And beautiful.

"I thought I would try to use the crutches today," she said.

David raised an eyebrow. "The doctor said a week."

"Well," she said with a quick grin, "it's been five days, a work week."

David shook his head slowly, his own mouth responding in a wry smile. "I take it math was never your subject. It was Saturday when they set that leg."

"Late Friday night," she countered.

"I'll compromise," David said. "If Sheila approves, we'll try it tomorrow."

"If I leave Thursday . . ."

"If . . ." The word hung in the air, and David's breath caught again. There was a hesitancy in the word, as if she had been reconsidering, and David felt a rush of adrenaline, of anticipation along with new apprehension. He wasn't entirely sure how long he could keep his hands away from her, particularly when she looked at him as she now was.

"I still . . . have the story to do. . . ."

"And I have a lot to show you." His words were carefully spoken. He wanted to say something entirely different, something like "I want you to stay. . . . I'm not sure I can let you go."

But the words stayed in his throat as he commanded them to. He nodded. "In the meantime, I think I'd better get you downstairs to breakfast or we'll be late."

Laney tensed as he reached for her because she knew exactly what would happen. Her bones seemed to liquefy, and her senses spun out of control. She tried to hold her body a little away from his, but it had a will of its own, and she felt herself snuggling up to him, her head tight against his chest, where she could hear his heart beat. Her arms had gone around his neck, and the thick hair tickled her skin, and her hands tingled where they touched his skin.

She looked up and saw a muscle jerk in the hollow of his cheek, and felt the tautness of his body. His moss-green eyes were curtained, golden-brown lashes shading them from intrusion. Yet his hands were gentle, as if he were holding a treasured and fragile object.

Laney had never felt fragile until now, had never wanted to feel fragile, but there was something undeniably wonderful about that feeling now.

There was magic in it. Laney felt like both Cinderella and Snow White, heroines whose princes represented both love and danger, awakening and loss.

They'd had happy endings, but Laney couldn't envision a happy ending with David. She and David were worlds apart in so many ways.

They reached the kitchen, where lovely smells filled the warm, noisy interior. Like the day before, there were fresh biscuits and jam and eggs and slabs of ham.

But Laney's appetite had fled, her stomach too filled with butterflies to welcome anything substantial. She listened to Abe and Theo chatter about the school party the following day and how "major awesome" it was that Laney was accompanying them that morning. Their pride sent little jolts of pleasure through her until she met David's eyes and saw warning signs there.

Don't get too close to them, they seemed to say, and the warning hurt. Her brief joy faded in the silent rebuke.

The bite of biscuit lodged in her throat and she felt a tightness behind her eyes. Uncertainty fogged her mind, and almost blindly she moved suddenly, knocking a fork from the table.

She reached down for it, just as David did, and their hands touched, burning at the contact. Their eyes met, and suddenly the reserve was gone from his, and there was raw, hot hunger that reached out and seared her.

His hand clasped the fork, and then dropped it as abruptly as she had, as if he could hold it no more surely.

"Hey," Theo said, and the silent moment shattered. There was vulnerability and pleading and charm in David's expression, and Laney's heart flipflopped as she straightened.

"What were you guys doing there?" Theo asked curiously.

David raised an eyebrow, mischief in his eyes.

"Hunting," he replied. The suggestive inflection in his voice found its mark in Laney, but not in his son, who simply looked puzzled.

"Doesn't take me that long to find a fork," Theo mumbled.

Abe pushed an elbow into Theo's side, a gesture Laney thought intriguing.

"Well, it don't," Theo protested.

"Doesn't," David said patiently. "And it better not take you much longer to finish breakfast, or we'll leave you behind."

Greed replaced curiosity in Theo's face, and he started eating again, but Abe's utensils stilled as he looked from his father to Laney, a surprisingly adult speculation in his eyes.

"You too," David said. "I'll go warm up the truck." His eyes rested on Laney for a moment and then seemed to force themselves away. He rose and looked warningly at the boys. "We'll leave as soon as I get back."

Laney watched as he pulled on the sheepskin jacket with the same easy grace he did everything. Muscles flexed in his back, and she, who already so well knew his physical strength, watched the compelling masculinity of the man who combined gentleness with power, who defied every notion she'd ever had about men.

Two more days. Maybe three. And then she would have to leave.

She looked around the room filled with pots and pans and school pictures and country crafts, and knew that she would miss this place more than any home she'd ever known. She would miss the voices and the teasing and the fond scolding and the smells and the warmth.

Two more days. Maybe three. Time, perhaps, to discover that fairy tales didn't really happen. Not to practical people like her.

Ten

The sprawling white frame school needed a coat of paint. It was also badly in need of a new roof; even Laney's inexperienced eye could see that.

But the children were like those in any place, their faces red from the cold, their voices and laughter drifting clearly through a silence that Laney wasn't quite accustomed to. She was a city girl, always had been, and noise was part of her life.

The silence of this high country had a sound of its own. The laughter seemed clearer, the song of birds cheerier, but then, Laney thought, everything had appeared brighter in the past several days, bright and shining.

She asked herself whether that image could quickly become tarnished. Prior to coming to Cade's Valley, she had been tired, and rest had renewed and restored her natural optimism and curiosity. David Farrar was only part of that refreshening. Nothing more.

Yet she felt a nervousness and even a kind of stage fright as he helped her into the wheelchair that had been placed in the back of the truck. David also dropped a guitar case in her lap, and ignored her questioning look.

A guitar? At school? But David must know what he was doing. He always seemed so sure of himself, and she knew he must be a fine teacher. She was struck with the old insecurity that had plagued her as an adolescent and that still haunted her. She'd always felt that one day she would wake up, and her career, her accomplishments, would be gone, punctured like a balloon, nothing more than a dream she'd conjured in a small, dingy furnished apartment.

Which was why her editor's criticism had hit her so hard. She could see everything going up in smoke. It was the main reason, she told herself, why she'd agreed to come to Cade's Valley and then to stay with David Farrar.

"You'll like them."

The words pierced through her thoughts and she realized again how easily he read her. She looked up and saw mischief dancing in his eyes.

"I'm an outsider, remember."

"But a very pretty outsider," David replied. "Did I tell you how nice you look?"

Laney grimaced as she looked at her encased leg. "I feel like an elephant with this on."

"Believe me, Miss Drury, you resemble nothing like an elephant. A gazelle, maybe."

The image pleased her immeasurably, and some of the uncertainty left her as she cocked her head and turned to look up into his face.

Her heart started thumping as she saw his wry grin, as if he were regretful about his own words. Laney felt vulnerable again, unsteady and unsure.

She felt even more unsure when she entered the school and saw the way the hurrying children sent curious glances and grins toward David. This was his ground, and not hers, and she wished for a moment he could see her at her best, doing what she did best.

She was pushed into a large room divided into three sets of chairs—one for each of the grades he taught—and she saw Abe already seated. Heads turned when she and David entered. The noise quieted and anticipation filled the room.

David pushed her to the center of the room. Instead of introducing her as she'd expected, he reached down and took the guitar out of the case in her lap. He leaned against his desk, folding his long legs, and a faraway look came into his face.

In a low but compelling voice, he began to sing.

Ye gentlemen and ladies fair who grace this famous city,

Just listen if you've time to spare, while I rehearse this ditty;

And for the opportunity conceive yourselves quite lucky

For 'tis not often that you see a hunter from Kentucky.

I suppose you've read it in the prints, how Packenham attempted

To make old Hickory Jackson wince, but soon the scheme repented;

But Packenham he made his brags, if he in fight was lucky.

He'd have our girls in cotton bags in spite of old Kentucky.

Old Hickory led us to the swamp, the ground was low and mucky,

There stood John Bull in martial pomp, and here was old Kentucky

But steady stood our little force, none wished it to be greater,

For every man was half a horse and half an alligator.

David's voice had grown more dramatic until the third verse, which he sang with a smile. The classroom was silent as he finished and cocked his head.

"Now, who can tell me what this song is about?"

Three hands went up, including Abe's. David selected a young girl.

"The War of 1812," she claimed.

"And what city?"

"New Orleans . . . the Battle of New Orleans," said another voice triumphantly.

"And Old Hickory?"

"Andrew Jackson," came the reply.

The questions went on, each one eagerly answered in a give-and-take discussion that even had Laney on the edge of the chair as David told how Jackson and the pirate Lafayette joined together to defeat the British. He was a natural actor, and he carried his audience with him, provoking thoughts and opinions.

An hour later David closed the topic. He introduced Laney. "I know you've all been wondering . . ."

Laney instantly knew what he had done—increased interest by making her, at least temporarily, a mystery.

"Miss Drury is a newspaper reporter with one of the finest newspapers in the country," he said. "She's been covering one of the presidential campaigns. Who wants to guess which one?"

Laney had to grin at his tactics. Shamelessly manipulative, she thought, for the guesses were coming hot and heavy and she immediately learned this particular class was a great deal more informed than most.

"Now, who would like to ask questions?"

They all would, she soon discovered. She had been worried about making a short speech in front of the class, in front of him, but she didn't need to. The kids leapt from one subject to another, asking questions that would do credit to a seasoned reporter.

The time sped along, and Laney was amazed at how much she enjoyed each moment. She looked up at David, and he winked, as if saying *Gotcha.*

And then it was lunchtime, though it seemed only minutes since she'd entered the classroom. In the lunchroom his students all wanted to know if they could sign her cast, and she told them she'd be honored. Drawings and a big Christmas tree, decorated with popcorn and paper links and painted eggshells, standing proudly in one corner, gave the otherwise barren-looking room color and warmth.

Laney's reporter's eyes noticed that much of the children's clothing was patched or too small or too large, and that all the food on the plates disappeared quickly. There were no leftovers.

David's glance followed hers. "Free lunches, for the most part," he said in a voice so soft only she could hear. "The mothers prepare and serve it."

She nodded.

"Have fun this morning?" His question was a little cautious, as if he were unsure of the answer.

Her answer had no caution in it. "Oh, yes," she said, and then grinned at the sudden pleasure in his face. "And you're a shameless ham."

"I am, aren't I," he agreed with a self-satisfied smile. "Beats banking by a mile."

"So that's why you teach? A frustrated actor."

"Minstrel," he corrected her. "Storyteller. Now, if I'd lived five hundred years ago, I would be a happy man."

She looked at his face, at the satisfaction in his

eyes and the mouth that smiled so easily. "I think you're a happy man now."

"I suppose I am," he replied seriously. "But it took me a while to get here."

"Will you tell me about your journey?"

"Still the ultimate newspaper reporter?"

"Partly," she admitted.

"And the other part . . ."

For me. Mostly for me. All for me. But she couldn't say that. She shrugged. "That curiosity I told you about."

"I like curiosity."

"Except when it comes to you."

"There's nothing mysterious about me. I'm a simple teacher, and I like what I do."

"You may be many things, Mr. Farrar, but simple isn't one of them."

He grinned. "Neither, my friend, are you. And if you open one door, we open both of them."

It was a warning, plain and simple. But any additional exploration of the subject disappeared with a ringing of the bell.

Laney sat outside, bundled up in a chair in David's yard. Despite the chill, she was warmed by a soft glow of contentment as her mind replayed the day.

The remainder of it had been as satisfying as the beginning. She had enjoyed watching him with the students, watching their response to him, the way he piqued their interest, whether it was math or English or geography. David held their interest by making each subject relevant to them, and he did it in a way to make them think. Near the end of the day, he suggested that the class develop a newspaper of its own and asked her for suggestions on how to go about it.

What she had done and said apparently pleased him, for as they drove home he discussed several of the students and their potential in a voice tinged with excitement for their futures.

At the house, after Abe and Theo had gone into their room to do their homework, David rolled Laney out to the backyard.

He grinned, with what could be termed only little-boy anticipation, and disappeared, returning with glasses of wine.

"You can't know these people and these hills until you see a sunset from here," he said. His hand fell to her shoulder as if it belonged there, and shivers ran up her back from the pleasure she felt.

She looked over to the mountains in the west, their tops glistening with snow, and the sun like a crown above. The sky was a deep royal blue, made lacy with clouds that sped across the crest of the mountains.

Laney took a sip of the wine, relishing the perfection of the moment: the crisp cold air, the satisfaction at the end of day, the touch of David's hand.

He moved closer and set down his glass. As both of his hands caressed her shoulders, the sky started changing colors, the clouds diffusing the rays of the sun until the landscape was painted with coral mixed with cinnamon and vivid red melding into purple. The colors were breathtaking, violent, and peaceful, clamorous yet compatible.

Like her feelings for him.

Almost as if his own thoughts were traveling the same path, he leaned down, touching his lips to her hair, to the base of her neck, where tremors started and raced through her.

"Thank you," he said.

Confused, she looked up at him.

"The kids . . . they thought you were great. So did I."

"I just followed your lead," she said. "Trouble was, I didn't have a guitar. Do you always start class with a song?"

"There's a lot of knowledge in songs, a lot of history and feeling." He hesitated. "Songs make history come more alive to kids, more immediate. It's no longer just a dry recital of facts, but real people who wrote songs about war and death, wandering and tribulations. They can relate to that."

His hand found its way inside the collar of her blouse, touching, sending little brushfires roaring along her nerves. The sky was all red now, a bright-burning crimson topping silvery-white peaks. It looked like a fire out of control, just as she was. Nothing mattered at the moment but his nearness, his touch, the magnetism that drew everyone to him.

And yet he, too, had his secrets. She sensed his fears were as strong as hers when she was away from him, when their proximity to each other didn't cloud reason.

David felt his hands doing things he'd promised himself he wouldn't. Yet he couldn't keep away from her, dammit.

She turned her head to look at him, and her eyes were incredibly wide, the color rich and deep with tiny flakes of amber. He leaned down and his lips touched hers. He'd meant it to be brief, but his lips hesitated and then responded to the yielding of her mouth.

He touched her cheek softly, and felt waves of tenderness cascade through his body. They had been building over the past several days, from the moment, he now realized, he'd first seen her in the wrecked car. . . .

He swallowed and straightened, his hand remaining on her cheek.

His voice was unsteady. "I'm afraid I'm about to destroy both our reputations."

She merely looked at him, her gaze challenging. "Do you care?"

He sighed. "Ordinarily, no, I suppose. In Boston, a kiss in public wouldn't make a ripple, but here it becomes a major event. Sort of on a par with the World Series."

"Or the Super Bowl."

"Or a catastrophic flood."

"News travels fast, huh?" Laney chuckled.

"Hell of a lot faster than your newspaper carries it," he said dryly.

"Cade's Valley's last remaining bachelor . . ."

"Almost," he agreed despondently.

"And everyone is trying to matchmake?"

"Everyone," he confirmed.

"And no luck?"

The smile left his face. "I don't intend to marry again."

The flat statement was like a bucket of cold water thrown in Laney's face. "Should I ask why?"

"Opened doors go both ways, remember," he warned.

But Laney needed to know more. At that moment she would trade anything to learn more about him.

"I remember," she said softly.

David looked out over the horizon. The sky had settled into a peaceful pink, the tip of the sun just barely visible behind the highest mountain. Dusk was falling quickly, and with it the temperatures. He felt her shiver under his hand. "Tonight," he said.

Laney felt her blood beat against her veins, the rhythm gathering speed until every sense was involved, seduced.

"All right," she said, and she blushed as she realized how hoarse her voice was, how tight her throat.

"It's going to be hell with you at the table tonight," he said.

"This doesn't make sense, does it?"

He smiled slowly, but there was regret in his eyes, even a certain grimness. "No."

Then Theo bounced toward them like an uncontrolled tennis ball, Laney thought. Just like Friday, when he'd run in front of her car. Was it just five days ago? It seemed a lifetime.

"Dinner's ready," he informed them.

"And you're through with your homework?" David queried.

Theo grinned. "Miss Davies didn't give us much. Aren't you cold out here, Laney?"

No, Laney thought. She wished she were. "Yes," she said.

Theo looked at her, then at his father, and winked at her. "Dad sure does like the outside." Then he was gone as quickly as he'd appeared.

Laney brushed her hair with unsteady hands, letting it fall over the gown and robe David had bought her. Dinner had been much like it was the previous night, full of conversation and questions, followed by more package-wrapping, then a game of Monopoly.

She'd never played the game before. Naturally competitive, she would have been absorbed in it if she hadn't been seated next to David, if his knee hadn't occasionally touched hers, and if his hand hadn't met hers at times, sending ripples of sensation through her. Their eyes had met, and held, almost as if they'd been hypnotized, until one of the boys or Mabel would jerk them back to reality.

Abe won the game, whether by steadfast attention or luck, Laney didn't know. David yawned, sent the boys to bed, and carried her up to the bedroom. He left to get her wheelchair, then disappeared, but with a promise in his eyes.

She waited as minutes went by, wondering what kind of fool she was. Hadn't Dean taught her anything? She'd grown up distrusting men, and Dean had proved her right. Hours earlier, David himself had said he would not remarry.

Why then was she waiting like a schoolgirl for her first date?

There was a soft knock on her door, one so light she knew he was probably having his own reservations.

Laney hesitated, thinking about playing possum, but the words spewed out before she could stop them. "Come in."

He'd changed into a pair of faded jeans that hugged his muscular legs and a sweatshirt that zipped up the front. The neck was open, and she could see a sprinkling of gold hair.

His hair was mussed, as if he'd been running his hand through it, and he hesitated at the doorway, as if reconsidering what they both had known, anticipated, and feared for hours.

"Tired?"

She shook her head.

He walked slowly over to the bed, and without words he took the brush from her hand and started stroking her hair with strong, sure movements.

"You have beautiful hair."

Each stroke felt like a finger running down her back, sending quivers throughout her body. He smelled of soap and a very masculine after-shave lotion, a spicy essence that was an aphrodisiac to her, just as everything about him was. Even Dean never affected her like this. She'd been physically attracted to him, but never in such a complete, elemental way. Together she and David were lightning and thunder.

David was playing with a strand of hair, and he rubbed it against her neck, his hand moving along her pulse and dipping toward her breast in a slow, seductive movement that electrified every nerve end in her body.

"I've been wanting to do that all day," he confessed, his breath playing havoc with what was left of her senses.

Laney leaned against him, feeling again that sense of belonging that she'd never felt before. It seemed at odds with all the pulsating sensations building to a crescendo within her. Yet with him, the calm and the storm went together.

I don't intend to marry again. His words came driving back at her. Why should they hurt? She had no intention of marrying either. Remember your father, she told herself. How he left your mother. And how Dean had lied over and over again.

Laney stiffened, and his hands went still.

She felt the thump of his heart, the warmth of his body, and she looked up and knew the pleasure of simply gazing at him. Suddenly nothing mattered except him. Her hands went up and around his neck; her lips lifted to meet his.

"Are you sure, Laney?"

She couldn't speak, only nod. She no longer had a will of her own. It was mixed somewhere with his, surrendered to the stronger need of their bodies.

His lips met hers, and hungrily they joined.

David knew this was crazy. But from the moment he'd touched her lips as the sun was setting, he knew it was inevitable. The knowledge had also been in her eyes.

Perhaps, he'd thought, their attraction was mere curiosity. Maybe they both needed to satisfy that curiosity, and then they could get on with their own lives.

He'd tried to stay away. He'd waited until the boys were asleep, and Mabel had retreated to her room on the first floor, and still he had waited, sitting with a brandy in his study, looking at the room as if he'd never seen it before. It was his, all his. His computer where he worked on his collection of folksongs, the books he'd so carefully collected, the photos of his boys. His sanctuary. He'd had a study in Boston too, but it had never felt like his. It belonged to Julia; her money had bought it, not his, and he'd gone along with it because the condominium had been so important to her, and she was already sick.

But he'd always felt a stranger there.

He wondered what kind of home Lane Drury had, and then he dismissed the thought as foolish. Laney wasn't like Julia; she had a career of her own, one she obviously enjoyed. And she must have worked hard to get where she was.

He couldn't ask her to give it up any more than he could give up what he had.

But, damn, she'd gotten under his skin quickly.

He'd risen, feeling the swell of desire rub painfully against his jeans, and he'd moved up the stairs and to her room.

When he'd seen her sitting on the bed, her hair brushed to a sheen, his hesitation disappeared. When he joined her on the bed and their lips met, his world exploded, all his self-control flying like shards from a fiery explosion.

She was twisted around now, her shoulder against his chest, her mouth linked to his, one of her breasts pressed tightly against him. Her hands were running through his hair, her long fingers playing enticing games with the sensitive skin of his neck.

His blood was like currents of liquid fire, searing

and sensitizing every nerve, every muscle. He'd never felt like this, never felt so electrified, so alive.

She whimpered as one of his hands entered the slit of the robe and moved farther down, stroking and caressing the satin of her skin, moving with wondering fingers across nipples and breasts that tautened. Pleasure coursed through him as she responded so completely to his every touch, her hands doing their own exploration, playing an equal part in an exquisite journey toward some unknown but desirable destination.

Despite the growing desire in him, he moved slowly, his hands gentle and cajoling rather than demanding. His physical need was overwhelming; it had been more than three years since he'd made love to a woman. But Lane was the important factor here, her pleasure, her well-being. From scattered impressions, the cautious reserve she had sometimes shown, he sensed she'd been hurt once. He didn't want to hurt her again.

Laney felt him tremble as his hands carefully explored her with restrained tenderness. She knew from the tension in his body how much that restraint was costing him. She knew because she also felt a terrible urgency, a need unlike any she'd ever felt.

Raw desire coursed through her, along with an overwhelming urge to give, to present David with a gift of her own, to give of herself in a wanton, selfless way. She wanted to see his slow, lazy smile, to watch his eyes glow with the same passion she felt. Her hand moved to his face, tracing the lines in it as their lips joined with a sweet savagery.

He moved slightly and she hated the cumbersome cast that allowed her so little movement, but it didn't appear to worry him. He deftly managed to slip off her robe and he bent his head to the opening of the gown, his mouth searching and finding the tip of one of her breasts. She could feel it swell and tighten with passion, and she cried out with pleasure. His tongue moved, teasing and stroking until her body quivered with waves of pleasure that swept away caution.

"Oh, David," she heard herself whisper.

"God, but you're pretty," he replied, "too close to perfection to be real."

Laney swallowed. No one had ever looked at her like this, had touched her as if she were incredibly precious. No one had ever said such words. She felt as if she were drowning, drowning in sensation, in wonder, in passion. His mouth joined hers with hungry urgency.

Her fingers shamelessly found the zipper to his sweatshirt and pulled the tab down slowly. She felt the wiry curls of chest hair, the hard muscle of his shoulders, the warmth of his skin.

His hands were moving with loving strokes over her hips, her stomach, his mouth trailing kisses where his hands had been until she could no longer stand the torment.

"I need you," she whispered. "I want you."

One of his fingers trailed down her stomach as he raised his eyes to meet hers. They were steady, but the green, usually so calm and comforting, was now glittering with a fire of its own.

Still there was a question in them.

"I'm sure," she whispered, and his lips crooked into a small grin.

"I'm not sure whether we'll ever recover," he warned in a hoarse tone that was sexy.

"I don't care," she replied recklessly. And she didn't. Nothing mattered except the consuming need to join her body with his.

He moved away slightly, unzipped his jeans, and quickly discarded them along with his briefs. He kneeled on the bed, and she looked up at him.

He was the most irresistible man she'd ever seen. His face was both rugged and gentle, his body rock hard. She let her gaze wander from the slightly troubled look on his face to his torso, and with trembling fingers she touched the lean line of his hip, the flat stomach, the blond hair that made an arrow leading down to where his manhood touched her skin.

Her hand touched the most intimate part of him, and she saw him tense. Then he slowly, carefully, moved, arching his body above hers.

Laney instinctively reacted, her own body curving up as much as possible, reaching to meet him.

She felt the first probing, throbbing touch of him, and she was swept with billows of exquisite yearning. She felt him enter, and the most intimate part of her tightened around him in a lover's embrace. His body started moving in a gentle rhythm and then gained in speed and tempo and strength until he was taking her to places unknown, to another universe of incredible pleasures, to a whirling kaleidoscope of dazzling colors and sensations, each stronger than the last until she didn't know whether she could stand any more.

But still his movements quickened, and she was carried along with him, a mysterious expectancy building within her until her body seemed to burst like flares of incredible brightness.

Laney clasped his back, not wanting to let him go, and she tasted the salty glaze on his skin as her tongue reached out to lick and savor the essence of him.

"Laney," he whispered, as slowly his body relaxed.

Eleven

Laney stretched languidly, and contented herself with playing with the tufts of hair on David's chest as he moved beside her, his hand on her waist as if he hated to stop touching her.

She cradled her head in the nook of his arm. It was a fine enough substitute for what she really wanted to do—to wrap herself around him—but the injured leg made it impossible. The cast had presented little problem in their lovemaking, now that she thought about it. . . .

Where there's a will . . .

She chuckled softly.

"Hmmmm, I like hearing you laugh, Laney." He drew out the name.

"I like hearing you say my name."

"You know this wasn't very smart."

"Nope," she replied happily.

His arms tightened around her. "Tell me more about you."

"What do you want to know?"

Everything, he thought. Had she ever been in love? How important was her career? What dreams did she have? But he was afraid to ask any of them. His body still felt seared from their mating. Mating? No. They had made love in the truest sense of the word, each giving, each sharing. He'd not known love could be like this.

And she would be gone in a few days.

"How you live in Washington," he finally answered. "What you enjoy doing in your free time. What kind of books and music you like."

"Important stuff like that?" Her tone was slightly mocking, as if she knew he was avoiding the real questions.

His hand teased her ear. "Yeah. Important stuff like that."

"All right. I have an apartment that I've never really lived in. Second, I don't seem to have any time off. I like all kinds of books and all music with the exception of heavy metal. And now it's my turn to ask a question."

"Bad bargain," he complained. "I didn't get much."

"You didn't ask the right question."

"And what is the right question?"

"You've already lost your turn."

He grumbled. "All right," he finally said in a resigned but wary voice. "Ask away."

There were so many things she wanted to know about. His wife. His vow not to marry again. Whether he planned to stay in Cade's Valley forever. But she couldn't form the words. She was afraid of the answers.

She did what he'd done—turned coward. Her reportorial skills had just gone to hell in a handbasket.

Laney turned her face up toward his, her mouth creasing into a grin. "What do you do in your time off? What books do you read?"

David's chuckle started deep in his throat, and Laney thought she'd never heard such an attractive sound. "We're both tiptoeing around the real questions, aren't we?"

She nodded, her hand entwining with his.

"Like what happens when you leave?"

She nodded again, her hand tightening.

David wanted to ask her whether she would consider returning to Cade's Valley, but there was too much fear in him. Fear for his boys, who'd had enough grief, who'd lost one mother. Fear for himself, for finding himself once more torn between love and a profession that was, for him, a calling he couldn't deny.

"What do you want, Laney?"

She grimaced. "I thought I knew. I wanted to be the very best. I wanted what I have, and then I wanted more."

"What?" The question was gentle.

"Washington bureau chief," she said. "I knew it wasn't possible with my paper. There are too many others in line, but I recently interviewed with another paper." She shrugged. "I haven't heard anything, but perhaps that's because my writing hasn't been up to par lately." She was surprised at how easy the admission came. She would never have said that to anyone else.

"Would that make you happy?"

"I don't know," she said honestly. "I'd thought so. There's so much more power there, decision making, independence."

"And you like independence?"

Laney lay quietly. "My mother struggled all her life, suffered all her life, because she depended on a man who ran out on her. I'll never let that happen to me."

David hesitated. "And you've never been in love?"

Not until now, she wanted to cry out. "I thought I was," she said instead.

"And?"

"He lied to me about his marital status."

So there it was, David thought. Two betrayals in her life, both by men. No wonder she cherished the thought of independence. No wonder she'd been so careful.

"And children?" For some reason, David felt his own breath catch.

Laney was silent, but she squirmed slightly in his arms. That was the rub. She wanted children. She wanted them badly, and perhaps that was why she'd been so vulnerable with Dean. It had seemed so perfect. Two reporters who understood each other, who understood the demands of that career. Marriage, for the first time, had looked feasible. She could have it all.

But you could never have it all! Laney had learned that the hard way. You made choices. And then you lived with them the best you could.

She buried the hurt, the part of her that wanted and longed for children, and she kept her eyes away from David as she finally responded. "With my job? I've been in my apartment five days in the past three months."

"And your job is so important?"

"Yes," she said fiercely, trying to convince herself. She'd never had to do that before. Reporting had always been her life, her future.

Something died slowly in David, the glimmering of hope he'd been harboring all day, ever since he saw her in class, the way she'd been with his kids.

"You're good with children," he said, but the reserve was back in his voice, and his hands had stopped kneading her arms.

She turned around and looked at him, her smile so shy and insecure that it nearly broke his heart. "Do you really think so? I've never been around children much. I wasn't sure."

"Abe and Theo were captivated a while back," he said dryly, "and my class was today." She had ensnared him days earlier, but David wasn't going to admit that, not with her planning to leave.

"I can see why you get so much pleasure from them," Laney said, turning her head to stare at the wall again. She couldn't bear watching the dimple that had suddenly appeared in his cheek. She wanted so badly to kiss it.

"Do you?" There was a twinge of something like bitterness in his voice, and Laney was startled by it. He always appeared so confident of himself.

Laney was silent, knowing he would continue in his own way and time if she allowed him to.

His voice was deep and anguished when he finally spoke. "My wife hated the idea of being married to a teacher. In her mind, a man taught only if he couldn't do anything else. It represented failure to her."

Laney heard the deep pain in the words, and she hurt desperately for him. She knew him well enough to understand his pride in his work as a teacher. To be considered a failure by someone he loved when he so excelled at what he wanted to do must have been terrible.

"Tell me about her," she said.

"Julia? She was breathtakingly beautiful," David said slowly. "You had to keep looking to make sure she was real."

Laney felt her stomach knot. She was attractive enough; she knew that. But beautiful? Her chin was too jutted, her cheeks too angled, her eyes too large. She had a certain appeal, but no one had ever called her beautiful, not until David.

"She was like a princess," David continued slowly. "A fragile princess who'd always had whatever she wanted."

"And she wanted you."

"I never thought I had a chance, so I didn't even try," David said. "I guessed later that was what appealed to her. She wanted what she couldn't have." The bitterness was gone now, replaced by a lingering sadness.

"Is that when you went to Boston?"

"Not right away. She said she would go anyplace with me, do anything. I took a teaching job, something like this one, in another community, and she hated it. When Abe was born, she went into a deep depression, and I promised I would give Boston a try. Her father had tried constantly to get me into the bank. It was largely family-owned, and Julia was his only child. He and his wife adored her.

"I tried for two years," David continued in a low voice. "I knew almost immediately it was a mistake, but then Theo was on the way, and after his birth we discovered she had cancer. I couldn't leave then. I couldn't take her away from her family, and I couldn't leave her, not when she was sick."

"It must have been terrible for Theo and Abe."

"It was. One operation after another, each one leaving her weaker. But she fought hard, mainly because of them, I think. She loved them. She really loved them." There was a subtle emphasis on the word "them," and Laney heard the loneliness and grief in his voice. Her hand reached out to his and took it, feeling the way his fingers tightened around hers, as if she were a lifeline.

"So you came back to teaching."

"For me. For the boys. They needed to leave that house with its memories."

"So did you," Lacey observed.

"I never liked it. It sat like a castle in the sky, surrounded by cement. It never seemed real to me, like a home. Maybe I never tried to make it one."

Laney found that hard to believe. David Farrar

seemed the type of man who would make the best of anything.

As if he read her mind, he continued, his voice tinged with regret. "I wasn't a . . . very good husband. I resented Boston, and Julia knew it. We fought about raising the boys, about money, about her family, but it was really always about the fact that I wanted to come back here. I just couldn't give her what she wanted."

"And she couldn't give you what you wanted," Laney said. "That's not anyone's fault."

"It was mine in not realizing how different we were," he said. "How wide the gulf was between what we each wanted. The marriage was a mistake."

"But you have the boys," Laney said, her heart cracking as she read the message in his words.

"Yep," he said, and his voice was lighter. "I have the boys."

Her fingers ran along the back of his hand. Such a strong, sure hand. On impulse she brought it to her mouth and kissed it, letting her tongue tease the tiny blond hairs that contrasted with the bronze hardness. She wanted to take the grief from his voice, the hollowness from his words, the loneliness from his eyes. They didn't fit him, didn't fit the strength that radiated from him. Or maybe they did. He was a man who felt things strongly, who did everything passionately, who loved deeply. She could only imagine his agony when his two loves conflicted so bitterly.

But he'd gone on. He'd probably been successful as a banker, because he would bring that personal dedication to anything he did.

Laney felt tears well in the back of her eyes. How could one fall in love in such a short time? How could one be sure it wasn't only physical attraction or emotional need? That had been what it was with Dean. She knew that now, just as she knew her pain had come mostly from wounded pride rather than lost love.

She knew because what she was feeling now was something altogether different. So much different and so much deeper that it frightened her.

Yet she couldn't let go of David, not of his hand, not of his sudden trust, not of his sharing what she knew had been hidden for a long time.

And she understood, as she had not before, his hesitancy over the news story. He was an intensely private man who had suffered, and because of that he had a rare compassion. He understood the people in his community as few outsiders ever could.

Laney knew suddenly she could give him a gift. That it might be a farewell gift was an excruciatingly painful thought. Yet, there seemed to be no alternative.

He had made it clear that he didn't wish to marry again, and now she understood why. And even if that weren't the case, she wasn't sure that she could adjust to a quiet life in the country. She'd been on the fast track too long, had been independent too long, had been a city person too long.

She twisted around and kissed him, her lips touching his with bittersweet longing.

Their mouths melded, the mad, crazy urgency gone but the passion still there, like electricity in the air. Laney continued to tingle with the feel of her body against his, held so tightly against him that they might have been one, still joined.

"Why don't you stay through Christmas?" he asked abruptly, as if the words exploded from him without thought.

Laney didn't answer immediately. She wanted to stay. Dear God, how she wanted to. But it would be a big mistake. It was almost impossible to leave now. What would it be like in a week?

"A few more days," she compromised. She needed a few more days anyway to accomplish what she'd just decided to do. "Will you take me to the cooperative?"

His hand brushed her cheek. "If you want to go. There's not much there, just an old warehouse."

"And to the party tomorrow at the school?"

"If you'd like."

"I have to call the office tomorrow," she said cautiously, "and make arrangements for a photographer."

He stiffened slightly. "Not any of the kids."

"Anything you say," Laney said airily, knowing that if she looked, she would find suspicion in his face. But she knew David would approve of what she planned to do. She hugged that thought even as she felt his withdrawal from her.

"I'll ask Sam if he can drive you over to the school tomorrow for the party," he finally said. "I know he plans to go. Sarah is helping with the lunch."

"And will you show me the rest of the valley?" she asked, touching him intimately.

"Hmmm," he mumbled. She was making him an offer he couldn't refuse.

David was gone from the bed when Laney woke up the next morning. The day was gray, the light barely filtering through cheery yellow curtains. She stretched out lazily, feeling extraordinarily content. If it hadn't been for her leg, Laney thought she could pull a Peter Pan and fly right through the window with exuberance.

She was going to stay a few more days. She wouldn't think beyond that.

Laney sat up and eyed the wheelchair, then the crutches. She wanted to try the crutches so she could go up and down the stairs on her own even though she hated to lose the benefit of David's arms.

As if summoned by her very thoughts, a knock came at the door, and when she responded, David came in, a tray in his hands.

Laney immediately thought of her tousled hair and sleep-filled eyes, but it was too late to do anything about them. So she merely let her gaze feast on him.

As if a Christmas gift himself, he was festive and bright. Freshly shaved and his hair still damp from a shower, he had dressed in a red sweater and tan slacks.

"Good morning," he said, a pleased-with-himself smile on his face as he set the tray down on the bed.

Laney couldn't keep a grin of her own from spreading across her face. He was so darned irresistible, she wanted to . . .

But she couldn't, because right behind him came Abe and Theo, both humming with excitement. And behind them were the two dogs and Long John, who jumped on the bed and eyed her tray with unblinking green eyes.

David looked around contritely. "I didn't mean to bring an audience."

But even as the words came out, Theo sat on her bed, a biscuit in his mouth. "Dad said you were coming today. That's really great."

Abe nodded in his own serious way.

Henry barked. Long John stared. David groaned.

"Out," he commanded to the boys. "You can see her later. In the meantime, why don't you finish packing the truck."

The two boys disappeared as quickly as they had appeared, along with the dogs. Long John stayed, his eyes still on the plate heaped high with biscuits, two fried eggs, and sausage.

"Long John," David scolded, but it didn't have the

same effect it had with his sons. The cat stayed, only swishing a tail in response.

Laney grinned. "The voice of authority."

David's scowl turned wry. "You've found me out. Ineffective. Completely ineffective."

Laney's smile grew broader. "I wouldn't say that." Her heart thumped with memories of the previous night.

"What *would* you say?" David's eyes gleamed as he leaned against a wall, his legs crossed at the ankles.

Laney looked at the cat. "We have company."

"Long John and I have an understanding. He doesn't rat on me and I don't rat on him." David's voice took on a sinister edge.

"Rat? Fine expression for a teacher."

David glanced at the cat. "But it fits."

Laney giggled. David had an outrageous sense of humor, always surprising her with its whimsy. He made her feel silly. Silly and in love.

So terribly in love.

"Dad." Abe's voice came from below. "We need help."

David ignored the plea. "Did I tell you how pretty you look in the morning? Especially when you're sleeping," he added roguishly.

"Dad!" The summons seemed to echo in the room, but David didn't move.

Laney managed to conquer the lump in her throat at the seductively spoken compliments. "When did you leave?"

"Just in time for propriety." He chuckled.

Laney felt her face flush. She remembered what he'd said teasingly on their drive from the hospital, that Mabel would stay because of reputations. She'd never lived in a small community, but she could imagine how gossip might spread.

"You look even prettier when you blush," he said,

and Laney felt like anything but a woman of the nineties.

"I never blush," she denied.

In three strides David was next to her, his face touching cheeks that were burning. His fingers caressed them gently. "Thank you," he said.

Laney knew he meant the previous night, and she felt tongue-tied all of a sudden. His nearness was an aphrodisiac, and nothing else was important. Not at this moment.

"Dad!"

David rose. "I'm afraid we'll be invaded again. Why don't you eat and clean up while I finish packing the truck? Then I'll take you downstairs."

Laney could only agree with a nod. She didn't trust her voice to be any more than a squeak at that moment.

David looked at the cat. "Should I take Long John?"

Laney swallowed and recaptured her voice. She knew how empty the room would be when he left. "You say he doesn't rat on his friends?"

"Never," he assured her.

"Then he may stay," she said primly.

"I might have to have a secret word with him," David quipped.

"It won't do any good. I intend bribery of the most blatant sort," Laney flipped back.

David leaned down and kissed her, then quickly straightened, and without a backward look he disappeared out the door, closing it gently.

Laney looked down at the tray. There was a warm cloth to wash her hands, and enough food to feed an army. There was even a somewhat malformed artificial rose, and Laney immediately thought of Theo. That was a Theo rose. An enthusiastic but haphazard product. Abe's would be perfect. She smiled at her own whimsy. Everything made her smile that morning.

She shared her breakfast with Long John, who wanted to be coaxed, although his fixed glare made it very clear he thought the breakfast was rightfully his and begrudged her every bite. Not that she wanted much. She felt giddy. In the past few days her world had been turned upside down, and after the previous night she knew it would never be the same.

Laney brushed her hair and washed in the large bathroom. She looked longingly at the tub, but that pleasure was days, even weeks away.

With disgust, she regarded her encased leg. How much she'd wanted to wrap herself around David as they'd made love. How much she wanted to take a long walk in the woods with him. She'd be long gone before that was possible.

Discouraged, she proceeded to dress and was ready when David reappeared, his face red from the cold, his eyes bright and excited. "Sam Talley will be over a little later to help bring the remainder of presents," he said. "He said he'd be happy to bring you. Oh, and he gave me this number for you to call about your car. He had it towed over to Granite Ridge, where there's a good garage."

Laney had given little thought to her car. David had said he would take care of it, and she'd needed no better promise. But now, she knew, she had to start thinking about practical things: car repairs, insurance.

The problem was, the only thing she cared about right then was when she would see David again.

"Will many people be there today?"

"Practically the whole valley is coming," he said. "There will be school until noon, and then everyone's bringing over some dish or another for lunch. Sort of pot luck. And then afterward, Santa pays a visit."

"Who's Santa?"

David narrowed his eyes. "I don't give away important secrets like that," he responded huffily.

"So I have to wait and see?"

"Yep."

She'd smiled at the short answer he used frequently. "You sound like John Wayne."

"Eloquent, huh?"

"Marvelously so."

"Well, thank ye, ma'am."

They smiled at each other, thoroughly engrossed in their nonsense.

Then he seemed to shake himself. "Ready to go downstairs?"

Laney was sitting on the side of the bed. "Will you help me with the crutches?"

He hesitated. "To the door. No farther."

Laney nodded. He took the crutches, which had been leaning against a corner of the room, and helped her to her feet. "Don't put any weight on the leg yet," he warned as his arms helped balance her.

She took one step, then another, growing more confident as she moved, especially with David hovering next to her, his hand resting on her arm. She took two turns around the room, and then one of the crutches got caught in a piece of furniture.

Laney started to fall and frantically twisted her body toward the bed, taking David crashing down with her.

Twelve

Laney landed completely over David, her face next to his, and she heard a muttered groan along with the clatter of falling crutches. Her hands were completely wrapped around his body, the two of them pressed together tightly.

"Are you hurt?" they asked each other simultaneously.

Laney ached, but not because of her leg. She was pressed against him, the most sensitive part of her against his hardening manhood.

David was in agony from wanting her so damned bad. His arms captured the softness of her body as he remembered how perfectly they had fit together the previous night, how soft and giving she was, and he felt his entire body tensing again. He had sworn that morning that their lovemaking would not be repeated. They'd used no protection, and in Cade's Valley there was no way of obtaining any without setting the entire community talking. Everyone would know the bachelor teacher was up to something with his houseguest. David didn't particularly welcome the speculation or questions that would follow. In many ways, Cade's Valley was as puritanical as it had been fifty years before.

But none of his resolutions seemed to matter right then. If he'd thought a brief encounter would cure what had been ailing him since Lane Drury appeared in his life, he knew now exactly how mistaken he'd been.

Her eyes were wide and worried, her mouth puckered in concern about him, and David couldn't help but kiss her, reassuringly at first, then with hunger.

The sound of hurrying feet on the stairs, however, made him realize where they were and that it was getting late.

He knew his face was somewhat red when his two sons burst into the room, followed by Mabel.

"We heard a crash," Abe said as wide, surprised eyes surveyed his father and their guest entangled on the bed.

"You all right, Mr. Farrar?" Mabel asked, that familiar speculative look on her face.

"Did you break your leg too?" Theo chimed in with enthusiasm.

David cautiously tried to straighten without revealing the telltale effect of the tumble. "Laney was trying the crutches and fell. That's what you heard," he said. "And yes, I'm all right, and no, Theo, I didn't break a leg, and I wish you didn't look so happy at the prospect."

"Well, gee," Theo said defensively. "Then you can ride all over in a chair, and we could sign your cast just like we did Laney's, and—"

"And I think it's time for school," David interrupted as he glanced at Laney's amused face. He didn't feel amused at all—just plain hurt. "You and Abe and Mabel go on down. We'll be there in a moment."

"You sure you can handle everything, Mr. Farrar?" Mabel's question was innocent enough, but David cast a suspicious glance at the housekeeper. He didn't appreciate the gleam in her eye.

"Mabel!" David's voice was as authoritative as he could make it.

Mabel chuckled. More like a cackle, David thought unappreciatively. But she left, closing the door with a suggestive quietness.

Lane rolled over and laughed, a deep sound that threatened another rise in David's temperature. "I think we've been compromised," she said with glee.

With a wince, David looked down at the fullness in his trousers and shook his head slowly. "You, lady, are a walking disaster."

"But I'm not walking," she retorted.

"A moving disaster, then?"

She snuggled up to him. "Am I?"

"Oh, damn," he said, knowing this was no way to cure his most immediate problem. He looked down at his watch, his face suddenly tightening. "You have a way of making me forget everything."

"Good," she said, but at the same time she moved away from him and watched as he slowly unwound himself from the bed and stood up.

He looked mussed and incredibly sexy with passion still glinting in his eye. She stretched, testing her leg.

"Are you sure you're okay?" he said, his voice slightly unsteady.

"No," she said. "But not because of my leg."

He raised an eyebrow. "We'll explore that subject later. In the meantime, my lady, your mount is ready."

"I know," she giggled, eyeing his midsection.

"That's not what I meant," he reproved her almost prudishly, his face creased into lines of mock disapproval although his eyes twinkled.

"Then by all means let us descend in dignity," she said with equal primness as she marveled at her boldness. It was totally unlike her, but ever since she'd met him she'd been looser, freer than she'd ever been in her life.

He was choking on laughter as he leaned down and picked her up. "I might never get to school again with you around," he whispered.

But he would. Some of the spontaneous pleasure of the moment seeped away as she thought of how in a few days she would be but a memory.

The laughter faded from her as he carried her down the stairs. The twinkle was still in his eye, and his mouth was curved into tender, amused lines. A face to cherish. A face to love. A face to remember. Could she ever give it up?

She would have to. He had made that clear. Her heart thumped as he sat her down on the sofa, and then returned for the wheelchair, leaving it within her reach. She noticed he didn't include the crutches.

The boys apparently had already gone outside. Mabel was back in the kitchen. A door suddenly slammed, a rush of cold air bouncing in along with Theo. "Ready, Dad?"

David nodded. "Everything packed?"

Theo nodded and grinned widely at Laney. "See ya later."

David's gaze rested on her a moment, but for once the expression was hooded. Then he smiled slowly and drawled, "Yeah, see ya later, Laney."

And with another rush of freezing air, they were gone. But a warmth remained, and David's beguiling smile continued to heat Laney from the top of her head to the tip of the big toe protruding from her cast.

Her wheelchair pushed by Sam Talley, Laney couldn't contain her own excitement as she entered the worn schoolhouse. It was contagious.

There were all sorts of vehicles outside, most of them old. Her gaze quickly found David's pink pickup.

People, mostly women, were streaming inside, carefully holding containers or dishes. Aromas floated up from the covered dishes and mingled with that of the evergreen that hung merrily in the halls and lunchroom. Loud voices and laughter echoed in the room as children dashed toward the grown-ups who entered.

A mountain of packages lay around the Christmas tree. Laney recognized the paper, and some of the crooked bows that Theo had tied. Hers, she soon noted, were not the only eyes centered on the multicolored presents. Eyes that were hopeful, wistful, happy.

In comparison, Laney's morning had been full of uncertainty mixed with occasional despair. She missed David. The house was filled with him, with bits and pieces of him, but it wasn't enough, not anymore. She wanted to be with him every second.

That knowledge was daunting. Her apartment and her job seemed so far away and she felt as if she were in a nether land that was immediate but had no future.

But then she thought of David, and he was very real. Images of him kept darting around in her head. His wary look, his amused look, his tender look, his loving one. And the mischievous bad-boy look that was so darned irresistible.

Her anticipation in seeing him had mounted as the minutes had rolled endlessly on, interrupted only briefly by several calls, including one to her editor.

Laney had explained what she wanted to do, the new twist she wanted to take with the story, and he'd approved, pleased, he said, at her enthusiasm. A photographer would be there in two days. The story was still set to run on Christmas Day.

He had ended the conversation by asking whether she wanted anyone to check her mail or answering machine. Laney had suddenly realized she'd not given a thought to either.

"I'll call the apartment manager," she'd told him, and several minutes later she had. The manager was glad she'd called; he'd worried about her since she'd told him she should be back by now. And he would be pleased to check her mail and messages and call back later. Laney said she didn't know when she would be in and would call him back instead.

She then called the garage. Her car was repairable, the man said, but it would take two or three weeks to get the parts. What did she want him to do?

Laney had looked down at her encased right leg. She wouldn't be able to drive until the cast was gone anyway. "Go ahead," she said, thinking it might give her a reason to come back. She gave him the name of her insurance company and told him to do whatever was necessary.

As soon as she'd hung up, Sam Talley had appeared at the door, ready to take her, his wife, and Mabel to the school, and she quickly forgot everything else.

Once in the lunchroom, her eyes hungrily sought the familiar tall figure that had become so dear, but he wasn't in sight. And then she didn't have a chance to look anymore because there was a long line of people in front of her, each obviously waiting to be introduced.

"Been meanin' to come over and bring some cookies," one rawboned woman said. "Thought you might need some mendin' time first."

"Sure do hate it you got hurt here in Cade's Valley," said a younger, bright-eyed woman with a warm smile. "My Ralph done bragged about you at dinner last night, how you helped with the school paper and all. He said you might be here today. Brought this with me." She thrust a small package in Laney's hands. "Ain't much, but perhaps you'll remember Cade's Valley kindly."

It was the first of a number of packages that accumulated in Laney's lap. Some of them were wrapped in obviously used paper, one even in a piece of cotton fabric that looked as if it had once been part of a dress.

She looked helplessly up at Sam, who grinned back. "You were hurt in *our* community," he whispered. "It's the Valley's way of extending sympathy and hospitality."

Laney was overwhelmed. She couldn't even begin to open the packages, not with her fingers suddenly numb and with tears backing up in her eyes. These people had so little, yet they had taken the trouble to share what they did have with a stranger.

She looked down again at the mound of items. "But none of them have names. How can I thank . . . ?"

"That's not important," he said simply. "I think you thanked them just by the way you accepted them."

Laney wanted to protest. It wasn't enough. No one had ever done anything like this for her. But before she could say anything, a plate was set before her, and as aromas floated toward her, she suddenly realized how hungry she was. She'd eaten very little of the breakfast David had brought that morning.

Cade's Valley might be poor, but it didn't show in the plate in front of her. Or perhaps it did. There was one slice of turkey, and the rest was filled with delicious but more frugal items, foods that had probably been canned from summer harvests. Jars of homemade jellies and preserves were stretched over the table to go on feathery-light biscuits, green beans were laced with pork rind, and stewed tomatoes topped slices of bread.

But where was David? And Theo and Abe?

As if in answer to her question, a small group of children, including Abe and Theo, filtered into the front of the room, along with David and his guitar. In minutes, Theo's voice was singing "What Child Is This," accompanied by David's guitar.

Entranced, Laney listened as the clear, lovely notes quieted the noisy room, and everyone stopped eating, all eyes going to the small choir. Each note, each word, was haunting in its beauty, in its clarity, the guitar and voice melding perfectly. Laney's eyes went from Theo to David. They were looking at each other, so attuned that Laney's heart hurt.

Laney looked around the room, at the rapt faces, some with tears in their eyes, and she felt a wetness in her own. For the first time in a very long while, Christmas meant something to Laney, something important.

And then the song was over, and David's fingers went to a lighter melody involving a certain reindeer. The crowd stirred again, but the voices of children underlay it all, enhancing the mood, delighting the spirit. Every once in a while Laney would look up and her gaze would catch David's, and he would smile that breathtaking crooked smile with the dimples, and Laney's heart would skip and run wild.

Suddenly the music ended, and he was by her side, dragging up a chair. She saw Theo and Abe separate and sit with other boys.

"That was lovely," she told David, at a loss to say anything else.

"The best is coming," he said, his hand covering hers for a brief moment. Just as David pulled it back, Laney heard a "Ho, ho, ho."

All heads turned toward the door, and a huge man, dressed in red and sporting a long red beard, trotted into the room, a bulging sack on his shoulders.

Laney looked at the beard, then at David, who shrugged and whispered, "Damned if we could get him to powder it."

"Who is he?"

He grinned. "The local bootlegger."

She looked at him with disbelief.

"True," he said, his face all twinkling like Santa himself. "I swear."

The next hour consisted of scenes that would be forever etched in Laney's memory. At the behest of the red-frocked Santa, all the children left their parents and gathered in front of the tree. Gift after gift brought squeals of delight. The lunchroom became littered with paper as children ran to show their parents the gifts. Each received a jacket and gloves and pair of pants and a toy. The parents smiled broadly, some even with tears again in their eyes.

Laney felt David's hand resting on her thigh. She looked at him and saw an intense emotion, something like elation, in his eyes, and her heart constricted and ached until she wondered how she could bear it. She had never known anyone to care so deeply, to give so completely without asking anything in return, and yet be held back in other ways. *I will never marry again*, he'd said.

He had warned her, she told herself. *Don't let yourself get any more involved than you already are.* But it was too late. In a matter of days David Farrar and Cade's Valley had become her whole life. How had it happened?

The rest of the afternoon passed in a blur. David's presence crowded out everything else. She was barely aware of Mabel and Sam's wife, who'd been helping in the kitchen, and of children who came up shyly to wish her a Merry Christmas.

Laney traveled back to the house with Sam because it was easier in his car with the cast. David was leaning on the truck waiting for her, an expectant look on his face. He opened the door, and picked her up, leaving Sam to bring in the wheelchair and the armful of packages she'd been given.

Theo and Abe were already inside, and Henry barked frantically in welcome as David set her down on the sofa. Gertrude barked belatedly and Long John came and sniffed her before disdainfully turning away. Laney felt as if she'd come home.

Sam looked down at the packages he carried and then around the still-crowded room. "Where do I put these?"

David looked at Laney. "Do you want to open them now?"

Laney suddenly felt like a child again. "Now."

David grinned. "Lots of Santa Clauses today."

"I want to see too," Theo said, and crowded close to her.

Abe didn't say anything, but he moved to the other side of her as David cleared the table in front of her, and Sam set down the bounty. Laney looked at the pile first, and then at the boys beside her and the man across from her, and she felt a wild surge of happiness, of belonging. She unwrapped the first gift, a jar of peach preserves. And then there was a box of homemade candy, a small carved owl that immediately captivated her, an embroidered towel, a jar of pickles, a pouch of dried flowers that smelled glorious. As she went through them, David guessed at the giver.

"That's Mrs. Rose, makes the best darn pickles in the county. And those dried flowers, Mrs. Gibbons.

Ralph's grandfather made that owl. He can do anything with wood." She wasn't a bit surprised that he knew them all so well.

When she was through, she felt very rich. "I can't believe everyone did this."

"They all love Theo."

"But I didn't do anything anyone wouldn't have."

He cocked his head to one side. "That doesn't make any difference. *You* did it. And you're here at Christmas because of it."

She winced. "I think I'm here because I want to be."

"Are you, Laney?" His voice was suddenly very serious. "Are you?"

Laney looked him straight in the eye. She wasn't sure she wanted to admit how she felt, but his gaze was compelling. "Yes," she said softly.

"Good."

Theo was looking at them expectantly. "What d'ya think, Laney?" Theo asked.

"About what?" Laney said, glad of the diversion.

"Today," Theo said impatiently. "Didja have a good time?"

"You, Theo, you," David corrected him good-naturedly.

"Did *you* have a good time?"

Laney wasn't quite sure what Theo was getting at, or why he had such a gleam in his eye. "I think you have a wonderful voice."

"Oh, not that," Theo said. "I mean the lunch and Santa and . . ."

"I thought that was wonderful too."

"And Cade's Valley? Do you like that too?"

She nodded.

"Better 'n Washington?"

Laney saw David raise an eyebrow. "Theo, take Henry outside for a walk."

"But—"

"Abe, you take Gertrude."

"Awww . . ." Abe had obviously been listening intently.

"Now," David said.

"See you in a few minutes," Theo said, looking cautiously at his father before dashing out of the room with Henry beside him.

"I'm glad you came," Abe said shyly. "I'm glad you're staying for a while." Then he followed Theo.

"They're wonderful," Laney said, still a little confused by their interest.

"You've been into the sherry," he said teasingly.

Laney suddenly felt awkward. Despite his light tone, there was something very intense about his eyes, something probing, as he hesitated over his next words. "How *do* you like Cade's Valley?"

She swallowed. She liked Cade's Valley. She liked it very much, but he was asking her something else. And she was afraid to say exactly how she felt for fear of rejection. And then there was her own uncertainty, her own warring needs. She made her voice as objective as possible. "Everyone . . . has been really nice."

It was a terrible answer, and she knew it the moment she saw the light leave his eyes.

He had been sitting on the sturdy coffee table, but now he stood, strain in every movement. "Let me take your coat," he said, his voice impersonal, and Laney felt deserted as he took the car coat from her arms and hung it much too carefully in a closet.

"A glass of wine?"

She remembered the wine they'd shared the day before as they watched the sunset, and glanced involuntarily toward the window. "Thank you," she said.

"Is there anything else you would prefer?"

She shook her head, knowing that she had destroyed those precious moments of closeness.

He disappeared, but reappeared shortly with a glass of wine for her and a glass of a darker liquid for himself. From the smell and color, she guessed it was bourbon.

He put his drink down on the table and then, as if needing something to do, put fresh logs in the fireplace and set them ablaze. He moodily watched the flames as he retrieved his drink and took a sip.

Laney hunted for something to say, to break the silence, which was so uncomfortable, so pregnant with emotion. "Theo has a glorious voice."

David didn't look at her, but kept his eyes on the fire. The reserve Laney remembered so well from the beginning was back in his voice. "That's one of the very few things I miss about a big city. I can't give him the musical training I would like to."

"Does he want it?"

No," David's voice lightened slightly. "He prefers catching snakes and other odd creatures."

Laney shivered. "I can't say I share his preferences."

"They're not so bad."

"Only when they're in the next state."

The next state. The words hovered between them, and Laney instantly regretted saying them.

"When will you be leaving? Have you decided?"

"Friday," she said. She'd made that decision in the past few seconds. The sudden chill between them had dictated it. No sense in putting off the inevitable, in making herself, and him, miserable.

He nodded without comment, his eyes curtained like she'd never seen them.

Then the boys returned and their chatter about the day masked the new awkwardness between their father and their friend.

• • •

When Laney rose the next morning, her first thought was *One more day. Just one more day.*

Had he really been asking what she'd thought he'd asked yesterday afternoon? Why had she been so afraid to find out? But she had, and she knew that his pride, and his past, wouldn't allow him to speak of it again.

He hadn't stayed with her the previous night. He had, in fact, left abruptly after a rather curt goodnight. Only his eyes had seemed to warm and linger . . . as if he wanted to say something more. But he hadn't.

She reached for the crutches, determined to start using them today. No more wheelchair. She would be going home the following day, and she would need her mobility. She wondered whether she hadn't delayed trying them because she enjoyed being in his arms too much, and whether he hadn't pressed her because he enjoyed having her in his arms. Yesterday, the thought would have warmed her; today it troubled her.

Laney walked around the room several times, feeling more and more confident using the crutches, though she was surprised how quickly tired she became, and how sore they made her arms. It had looked so easy when she'd watched others.

She tried to concentrate on things she needed to do. She hadn't called her apartment manager yesterday to claim her messages. She had to start writing her story and put together ideas for a photographer. She wanted to see the cooperative. Learn a few more facts about Cade's Valley: population statistics, skills in the community, assets.

Laney sat down on the bed, reaching for a brush on the table. She'd washed her hair the night before in the bathroom basin; it hadn't been easy, but she'd been determined. She'd thought of that old movie *South Pacific* and had resolved to wash David Farrar right out of her hair. Unfortunately, she'd had no more success than Mitzi Gaynor.

There was a knock on the door, and Abe called out to her.

"Laney, are you up?"

Laney hoisted herself on the crutches, stumped over to the door, and opened it. Abe was standing there, his eyes bright. "We're going to go get a Christmas tree. You're coming with us, aren't you?" His voice held more excitement than usual.

Laney's heart melted at the expectant upturned face. "I wouldn't miss it for the world."

"Great. Breakfast is almost ready."

She nodded. "I'll be down in a minute."

She quickly dressed, once more running a brush through her hair and dashing on some lipstick. She took a deep breath and reached for the crutches. She'd try the stairs on her own. She didn't think she could bear to feel David's arms around her again.

She reached the top of the steps just as he started up. "Laney, wait," he said, and leaping two steps at a time, he was beside her before she could say she'd do it herself.

"I don't think you should do this," he stated.

"I have to. There are stairs in my apartment."

She saw his lips tighten at the reminder she was leaving soon. But not nearly as tight as her heart, she supposed, and she ached to have him insist that he carry her. But he didn't. He merely nodded, putting his hand on her shoulder. "I'll stay beside you."

It was an agonizing descent because she knew any wrong movement might send her tumbling down and because of his proximity. His cologne intoxicated her, or was it his presence? Several times, she felt his hand, strong and sure, press on her shoulder, steadying her, and she knew she could do anything with him at her side.

But she didn't want anyone. She didn't need anyone.

She stiffened, and his hand left her. Suddenly Laney felt lost. And so alone.

Thirteen

Laney's sense of loss faded in the merriment in the truck. Spurred by Christmas carols wholeheartedly belted out by her three companions, she found her own slightly off-tune voice singing along.

The day was bright. Patches of snow still lay on the ground and glittered in the sunlight. The temperature was freezing, but Laney, sandwiched between David and the two boys in the front seat, felt warm and wanted.

They wouldn't go far, David promised. There was a patch of woods not many miles away with some outstanding trees "just wishing" to decorate someone's home. Abe and Theo chattered about finding the "absolutely most perfect tree."

Selecting a tree from the wild was a new experience for Laney, who had several years before resorted to a small artificial tree.

As David drove, his hand frequently brushed hers, and she felt as if lightning were running through her. He evoked so many different emotions in her, so many different needs. And they ran helter-skelter in her mind.

But she felt so alive. And so afraid.

• • •

All those feelings deepened during the day. They did find the perfect tree and then spent the afternoon decorating it. Mabel made hot chocolate and popcorn, some of which they ate and some of which they strung on thread.

The ornaments all meant something, and Abe and Theo explained each one. There was one for each Christmas for each boy, with his name and year on it. There were those they'd made themselves. Some of the glitter was gone from these, but Laney realized they were just as precious, if not more so, than the store-bought ones.

After the tree was decorated, David drove Laney to the cooperative. It was a large building and had been part of the now-closed mining operation. Staffed by volunteers, the cooperative was stocked with everything from new and used clothing to canned goods and secondhand farm implements. The food, like the other items, was priced at cost but, according to David, was sometimes donated to a family in particularly hard circumstances.

A woman whom Laney judged to be in her eighties sat in a rocking chair, her fingers busy with crocheting. Her eyes lit up when she saw David and Laney.

"Business good?" David asked.

"Not with yer party yesterday," she said. "Got real lonesome here. Is this that pretty newspaper gal everyone's been talkin' 'bout? Heard she's leavin' us. That right?"

David grinned as Laney shook her head in wonder.

"Laney, this is Agnes Appleton."

Agnes smiled, winking at David. "She sure is pretty. You like Cade's Valley?" The last question was addressed to Laney, who was realizing the extent of everyone's interest in matchmaking David. But she couldn't help responding to Agnes Appleton's eager smile.

"Yep," she said, borrowing one of David's favorite responses.

"You'll come again?"

Laney hesitated as she looked up at David. "I don't know," she said hesitantly.

"You will," she said with perfect confidence.

"Agnes sees the future," David said.

Agnes rocked. "Our David thinks it's nonsense, but he'll see. He'll see."

Laney hobbled around the huge room a few moments longer, amazed at the variety of goods. "A kitchen sink, perhaps?" she asked.

"Look long enough and you'll find one," David said. Eyeing her crutches, he added, "I think we'd better get you back. You've spent too much time on those."

Laney said her good-byes to Agnes Appleton. "I'll see you again, miss," the old woman said.

Back in the truck, Laney was filled with questions. Wasn't Agnes too old to tend the store by herself?

David's head turned toward her. "There's about twenty volunteers who each work half a day a week. They all enjoy it, Agnes perhaps more than anyone. Gives her a chance to catch up on the news."

"But isn't it dangerous?"

"Here? In Cade's Valley? Nothing happens in Cade's Valley. It took me a year to discover I didn't have to lock up the house like Fort Knox."

"But—"

"Everyone sort of looks after everyone else here."

They were silent the rest of the way. When David had parked, he looked at her. "Have everything you need?"

She looked at him questioningly.

"The story," he explained.

She nodded. "I think so. Thank you."

So polite, she thought as her heart plummeted.

So cool, he thought achingly as he realized his life wouldn't be the same again.

But neither of them could say anything.

When Laney opened her eyes the next morning after a nearly sleepless night, she felt a nameless dread, as if she'd just lost a loved one. Then she realized something else was strange, not quite right.

Red-rimmed eyes went to the clock. There should have been more light filtering into the room by now. Her gaze focused on the window.

Snow. Wonderful snow falling in big chunks. Delight filled her. She reached for the crutches, rose to her feet, and made her way to the window.

The world was like a Christmas-card scene, pristine and lovely. She could barely see the mountains through the heavy snow, and the limbs of the trees in the yard were like great silent white ghosts dancing in a fantasy.

She heard a knock at her door. "Come in."

The door opened, and David stood there, that crooked smile on his face, the one she hadn't seen in the past twenty-four hours. "You're marooned. I called the airport, and it's closed."

Laney couldn't help an answering grin. For the second time in her life, an unexpected snafu in her plans was making her immeasurably happy. The first was a week ago. A week? A lifetime.

"I guess I'll have to make the best of it," she replied softly.

"Will it be so difficult?" His eyes were searching now, wanting a certain answer, and she gave it to him.

"No." But her eyes said much more than the short answer, and she saw his face relax.

"I conjured up the snowstorm, you know," he said matter-of-factly.

"I thought it was fate," she retorted.

"You don't believe in fate, remember," he said gently. "Nor magic or fantasy or fairy godmothers."

He moved over to her, and Laney leaned against him, feeling the strength of his arms holding her, and she felt wholly safe again. Safe and happy and where she should be.

"I'm beginning to," she said finally, swallowing hard. She tried to make herself remember why she'd decided to leave. But for the life of her she couldn't, not with the feel of his soft breath on her neck, not with his arms around her, not with the sound of his voice in her ear.

"I was thinking how much the world looks like a fantasy now," Laney said. "Perhaps that's all this is."

"Is that what you really think? Something not real?"

"Don't you?" she replied cautiously.

"I'm afraid it's very real." His hands tightened around her. "The last two nights have been miserable."

Laney looked up at him. "For me too."

"What do you propose we do about it?"

Laney looked at the heavily falling snow. "Now that it's been taken out of our hands?"

His hands tightened around her waist. "Stay, Laney. Stay through Christmas."

What determination she'd had died. She had listened to her head before, and had almost immediately regretted it. Now she would listen to her heart. Through Christmas. One magical Christmas. One miraculous Christmas.

"Yes," she said simply.

He leaned down and kissed her, his lips light and gentle against her cheek, her mouth. "We have something, Laney. Something special."

She raised her head and said something she thought she'd never say to another human being. "I'm frightened."

"Me too, Laney, me too."

That afternoon she called her apartment manager and collected her messages. Among them was a call from the newsmagazine where she'd interviewed for the bureau chief job. After she hung up, she stared at the phone for a long while.

Somehow, she knew exactly what the message meant. She sensed it in her gut. The job was hers. There was something very ironic about the timing since she'd been thinking of nothing during the past several hours but staying in Cade's Valley.

But now . . .

The job was everything she'd been working for all these years. Recognition. Authority. Independence. Proof of her ability. Proof of her worth.

The paper she'd written the magazine's number on crinkled in her hands.

She started to reach for the phone, then drew back her hand. She would wait to return the call. God knew, she had an excuse. An accident. A broken leg. Marooned in the mountains.

Coward!

She had asked for the job. If offered, she would be expected to give an immediate reply. And she couldn't. Not now.

Laney carefully folded the paper and placed it in her skirt pocket. She looked out the window and watched

David playing with his sons in the snow. David's warm gaze met hers, his eyes suddenly filling with concern as he saw her.

She quickly turned around and painstakingly climbed the stairs to her room. David's room.

Laney wrote her story. It was both one of the hardest and easiest stories she'd ever written. Easy because her heart was in it. Hard because she wanted it perfect. Absolutely perfect.

David came in to check on her, but she sent him away, insisting that she not be disturbed while writing. He didn't look as if he believed the only thing occupying her was the story, but he didn't say anything and left quietly.

It was nearly dinnertime when she used the modem on her portable computer to send the story to the paper. She wondered whether a photographer could get to Cade's Valley during the storm. She hoped this one would be more determined to get in than she was to get out.

Dinner was joyful, and Laney didn't question the contentment she felt. She merely indulged in the lovely sense of belonging.

And then night came, and David stayed with her, his touches tender at first, but becoming more passionate, more demanding, more hungry until they were both wild with a craving that had grown after two nights of denial.

Their melding was explosive, and the aftermath incredibly sweet as David held her for a long time and stroked her hair. "I swore I wasn't going to do this."

"I would have been devastated if you hadn't."

He chuckled, a warm sound deep in his throat. "You're the most honest woman I've ever met."

She snuggled closer to him, cherishing the feel of his body next to her. "I'm glad I didn't leave."

Contented silence hung between them, yet there were still unspoken questions and unspoken answers. But for now, neither particularly wanted to puncture the cocoon they'd spun for themselves that night.

Fourteen

The photographer came the following day, having rented a helicopter at the paper's expense. He asked if she wanted a ride back, and she didn't have to think twice. She gave him a very sweet "No, thank you."

She pointed out places he should photograph: the cooperative, the town's main street, Sheila in her small clinic, David's screened porch filled with wrapped presents due to be delivered Christmas Eve. David flatly refused to be in a single picture, but Henry managed to be included in one, his front feet on a package and his tail wagging. It was clear David still wasn't sure whether he approved of her writing her story.

And for some reason she didn't show what she'd written to him. Shyness perhaps. Maybe the story wouldn't run. Or maybe she just wanted his unqualified trust.

Christmas Eve was pure enchantment, from the moment Laney woke up in David's arms through the trip to the hospital. The roads had been cleared, and the scenery was breathtaking with its frosting of snow. While her leg was X rayed, David disappeared.

He came back to pick her up and to hear an excellent medical report, then took her shopping. Laney bought much-needed skirts and sweaters for herself, a book each for David and Abe, a game for Theo, and a scarf for Mabel.

After a festive dinner with Christmas music on the record player and watching *A Christmas Carol* on television, David read the boys "The Night Before Christmas," then tucked them in bed. With Mabel installed in front of the television, David dressed up in a Santa Claus outfit and he and Laney took the truck filled with the gifts from the porch. Laney snuggled herself into his arms, giggling when the beard tickled her.

"You ought to wear that all the time."

"I could grow one," he said helpfully.

"Ummm, don't you dare," she said. "It will be too difficult to do this." She leaned up and found a bare place in his face and kissed it.

"Be careful, lady," he said, "unless you want Santa arrested for lewd conduct."

She laughed. "It would make a great story. I could be front-page all over the country."

She started nibbling again, and he growled. "Laney, we're going to be in another ditch in a minute."

"All right," she said. "I'll behave. Briefly."

But she behaved longer than that, because his visits started. At each stop a woman or man or older child would open the door, sometimes coming out to the truck to greet her, their smiles grateful and happy. Laney felt a warm joy crawling around inside her that she was a part of this.

At one house, when David was carrying packages inside, Laney happily listened to "I Saw Mama Kissing Santa Claus" playing on the radio, and blessed her editor at her paper. He apparently knew her better than she knew herself. If anyone had told her six months before she would be spending Christmas Eve in a pink pickup truck in the middle of nowhere with a man sporting a waist-long beard, she would have had that person committed.

She ought to have herself committed.

They got home in the wee hours, and Laney did get her chance to kiss Santa Claus. Again and again and again.

Several hours later she woke and reached for him, but he wasn't there.

Her gaze went around the room and found him gazing moodily out the window, his long, fit body like a sculpture in the moonlight reflecting off the snow.

"David."

He turned. "The kids will be up soon."

"Don't leave yet."

He got back in bed and drew her to him, but some of the old reserve was there.

"Where do we go from here?" His question was immeasurably sad.

Laney swallowed deep. "I talked with my editor." She hesitated.

"And," he said softly.

"He liked the story about Cade's Valley. He wants me to do more of that kind of thing, which means I could live almost anyplace."

"I thought you liked politics."

"I thought I did too," she said wryly. "But I haven't been so sure lately."

He stiffened, waiting for her to say more.

"There's something else," she said, determined now to tell him everything and discover his reaction. Did he want her? Did he really want her? It had been such a short time, yet fantasy had become reality and reality fantasy. This was where she belonged.

"What?" he said, expelling breath that had been

lodged in his throat. He had hoped for this, but it was something she had to decide on her own. She had to be sure. He had to be sure.

"The job I told you about. The bureau chief. I think it's mine if I want it."

David's heart stopped. She had made it clear that job was the pinnacle of what she'd strived for, what she wanted. All he could offer was a small house, a community without stores, a teacher's pay, and two kids. How long would it take her to grow restless?

"David?"

"I'm happy for you, Laney," he said, and rose. "The kids will be up at the first ray of sun."

Laney blinked back the tears as he quickly dressed and started for the door.

"David," she said again, and he stopped moving. "Merry Christmas."

His face gentled. "Merry Christmas, Lane Drury."

Norman Rockwell would have had a field day, Laney thought, as he looked around the living room.

Two towheaded blue-eyed boys sat among ribbons and paper and boxes as their father winced at both the largess and the mess. She already knew that he was not altogether happy about the number of packages from the boys' grandparents, but he didn't feel he had the right to limit them.

So he looked on indulgently as the paper piled higher and Henry and Gertrude and even Long John sported big red ribbons around their necks. The only missing element was Mabel, who was spending the morning with her family, but she would be over later. Abe had solemnly served as Santa's elf, delivering packages to the right people. Laney herself had a little pile next to her, but she treasured them, not wanting to open them yet, protracting the delight and curiosity.

When Abe and Theo had opened all theirs, eyes turned to her expectantly.

She opened Theo's first, obvious by the childish scrawl of her name. His anxious face looked at her as she revealed a handmade billfold, parts of it a bit lopsided but obviously constructed with care. Her cry of pleasure set Theo beaming. Abe's offering was a drawing of the mountains, and it was, in Laney's eyes, quite wonderful. From Mabel, there was a knitted scarf, and Laney wondered only briefly when she'd had time to do it.

And finally, David's. It was a tiny box, and she opened it slowly and carefully, cherishing every second. She couldn't stop a smile of delight as she found a necklace, a gold chain with an exquisite small gold unicorn. David's fantasy. David's magic. The magic she'd finally started to believe in. She felt her throat grow tight, her heart pound erratically as she noticed that his own eyes were as anxious as Theo's had been. Dear Lord, how she loved him, but how could she convince him?

Perhaps the story. They had already opened her presents, and David's hand had lingered over the leather-bound copy of *David Copperfield*. But she had something else too, something for David.

She had debated giving it. Uncertainty had rocked her while she had dressed that morning. What if David didn't like it? What if . . .

"I have something else," she said shyly. All three faces looked over at her. She had buried the papers next to her, and now she handed them to David.

David look at her curiously, then began to read out loud. "Christmas In Cade's Valley."

"Time appears to have stopped in this lovely little valley nestled in Appalachia.

It could well be a hundred years ago in Cade's Valley, instead of Christmas in this modern age. It could even be two hundred years ago, when the valley was first settled by Jesse Cade.

There was a sense of community then, from what they say. There is a sense of community today. Of fierce loyalty to one another, to families, and to the beautiful rugged land that has been home to numerous generations.

Nothing has changed the instinctive hospitality, the natural urge to help through rough times, to share what little one has.

Cade's Valley has fallen on hard times. But Christmas brings a joy and generosity that beggars richer communities.

And it still has hope this Christmas, although that hope sometimes dims when young people have to go to another place to earn a livelihood. The people of Cade's Valley see their community disappearing, but they still have hope.

They have hope that some company, some corporation, some government entity, will see the true riches it has to offer: its people. . . ."

The story went on, and David kept reading, his eyes occasionally going to Laney, but they betrayed little of his feelings.

When he finished, he went over to her, his hands on her shoulders, and he leaned down and kissed her in front of Theo and Abe and Mabel.

"It sounds like you might like Cade's Valley," he said cautiously when he finished.

She could only nod her head.

"Enough to stay?" Theo asked, a grin on his face.

"That's my line," David growled with mock ferocity. "And one I think Laney and I should discuss in private."

"Will you, Laney?" Abe persisted.

Laney looked up at David. "I haven't had an offer yet," Laney said.

"Yes, you did," Theo claimed. "I asked you."

"And me," Abe echoed.

But Laney's attention was directed at David. His eyes were grave, and she saw the questions in them, questions that indeed had to be answered in private.

She was barely aware of movement in the room, of a cough, of an elbow hitting a side, of two boys sliding silently from the room.

David, a muscle throbbing in his cheek, sat down on the coffee table. Laney felt the heat from his closeness, but she saw the uncertainty in his eyes, the fear of making another mistake.

"Do we have something to discuss?" she said in a voice that trembled slightly.

"What about that job?" His voice sounded strained.

She tried to smile. "Better offer or not," she said, "I've decided to turn it down."

"Why?"

"Do you always ask so many questions?" Laney hated the way her voice quaked as she repeated the question he'd asked her so many times.

"I've had a good teacher," he replied with a small grin.

"Why?" he asked again as his green eyes reached down into the deepest part of her being, searching, wanting.

The words almost choked in her throat. They were so important, so very important. "Because . . ." She hesitated, and then went on in a stronger voice. "Because I—I want to start looking at sunsets. . . ."

His hand took hers. "Any particular sunset?"

"Well, there's a particularly nice one nearby." Her fingers moved in his hand, touching with such longing that she trembled. Rejection or not, she had to know.

David stilled. "I have so little to offer."

"You have so much," she said. "Love and laughter and music and—"

"Sunsets."

"And sunsets," she agreed.

"And that's enough?"

"But that's only the beginning," she said. She thought of the world he'd opened for her. Of silent beauty, of people who cared, of the unparalleled sweetness of lovemaking, of happy faces, of dreams, of . . .fantasies that came true. Because he made them come true. Through sheer force of will, he prodded and harangued and preservered to turn wishes into reality.

Laney had always thought her realistic world was the better one. She'd always scorned the dreamers. And she'd always been the onlooker, never the participant.

No more. She would never be just a spectator again. Now she wanted to dive into life, to grab and taste, to give and take, to . . . make a difference.

And now was the time to begin. Now was the time to take a risk, the first great giant risk. "I love you," she said, uttering the words for the first time in her life. She'd always been afraid of them before—with her mother, with Dean.

"Laney," David whispered. "Are you sure? Are you very sure?" He hesitated. "I caught a butterfly once . . . it was so beautiful and free . . ."

Laney felt the soul-twisting agony of the words. "I'm not a butterfly," she said slowly.

"What are you, Laney? What are you really?"

She searched his eyes. "I don't know," she said slowly, honestly. "I just know that for the first time in my life I feel I belong. I feel warm and happy inside."

A grin broke out on his face. "And . . . ?"

She grinned back. "That too."

"And my imps?"

"Them and maybe a few more," she said.

Joy slowly filled his face. Joy and a kind of peace she'd never seen there before. But he couldn't resist one last caution. "You're absolutely sure?"

"I think it's the only thing I've ever really been sure of," she admitted shyly, an admission quieted by lips so gentle and loving that Laney felt the whole world soften under their impact. The kiss deepened, and she saw sunrises, and sunbursts, and sunsets. She saw shooting stars and novas. She saw it all in those few moments, and she truly knew the meaning of living.

"Guess she's gonna stay," Theo said as if from a distance.

A dog barked. A cat rubbed itself against Laney's ankle, and she heard a chuckle as lips left her mouth.

"I love you, Lane Drury," he said, nuzzling her ear.

"Yep, guess she's going to stay," Abe stated.

"Will you marry me?"

"Yep, she's staying," Theo confirmed.

David leaned back slightly, a crooked grin on his face as he glanced at his sons before turning back to her. "Will you . . . ?"

Laney looked at the three expectant faces and saw love. Plenty of love. A miracle of love.

The greatest gift of all.

And an offer she couldn't refuse.

Epilogue

December 25

A Special Christmas in Cade's Valley

Christmas has always been much loved and celebrated in Cade's Valley, in its hollows and farms, in the tiny houses once a part of a mining operation now long gone.

But this year the residents of this unique piece of yesteryear had another reason to celebrate.

They learned last week that the state had decided to build a major recreational area here, a state park that will provide new businesses and jobs.

The project was announced after two years of work by the citizens of this community, people who decided not to let their town die. . . .

David placed a hand on Laney's stomach, delighting in the movement of the baby underneath.

His other hand lay down the copy of the *Washington Times* he'd been reading. "Not bad for your last column," he said with satisfaction.

"Oh, they'll still take an occasional Sunday piece," Laney said. Cade's Valley had become famous in the past year through her syndicated column. The series of features on Appalachia and its people was ending today. She didn't want the pressure any longer, the deadlines, not with her growing family. And she had just signed a new contract with a publishing company for three more of her children's books, all featuring two blond-haired blue-eyed boys, a three-legged cat, and Henry the dog. Gertrude had mostly retired from the series, being allowed to enjoy her old age in protected hibernation.

The David Farrar family already knew the baby was going to be a girl, and Theo and Abe were beside themselves with excitement. They had been charged with finding exactly the right name.

And now they had it. They had been bubbling with excitement all morning, and at last they were ready to present it.

"Merry," Theo blurted out.

"Because Laney came to us at Christmas," Abe added, giving a censuring look at Theo for rushing the solemn announcement.

David looked at Laney, and she warmed to the quiet joy in his eyes.

"It's perfect," she said, thinking that Christmas was always going to be the most wonderful time in a life now filled with wonders. "Absolutely perfect," she added, her gaze finding and locking on three beloved male faces, their cheeks indented by dimples.

"Perfect," David echoed, and it was obvious he didn't mean just the name.

*If you enjoyed THE GREATEST GIFT,
be sure to watch for Patricia Potter's
thrilling historical romance,*

LAWLESS,

*On sale in January 1992 in paperback
from Bantam FANFARE.*

In LAWLESS, Patricia Potter tells the dramatic and compelling story of a brave and
beautiful schoolteacher and the lawless out-
cast who becomes her protector. When Willow
Taylor refuses to sell her land to a powerful
rancher, legendary gunfighter Lobo is hired to
drive her away. But his attempts go awry as he
ends up rescuing members of her "family"
from disasters, including a fire. Worse, he's
shocked to discover that Willow is unlike the
heartless women he's known only too well. In
the following excerpt, Willow finds their mysterious savior lending a helping hand around
her broken-down property. Not knowing that
he's her enemy, Willow offers him a job.

He was at the ranch when she arrived the next afternoon. His shirt was off, and his bare chest glistened with sweat and seemed to glow with the sun as he wrestled with fence posts. Muscles rippled along the full length of his body as he moved, and Willow thought she had never seen anything quite as gloriously perfect. Like a Greek statue pictured in one of her books.

He was, she thought fancifully, nothing less than poetry in motion.

He had looked up when she had driven up, but then went back to his task with no further notice, his face as impassive as always. The twins bounced down from the buckboard and ran over to watch, their mouths obviously pursed full of questions. Even Estelle was on the porch, cautious but interested.

Willow watched as he finished the last railing, and she neared. He was wearing no gloves now, and his hands were still red and raw-looking. But she wouldn't know he was feeling any pain at all from the way he handled the tools.

He gave one last look to the fence, apparently satisfying himself that it was completed, and started for his horse as he fingered a pair of obviously new gloves. Willow plotted a collision path with him, and he stopped just seconds before he would have crashed into her.

She took his hands, preventing him from hiding them within the gloves he was holding, and her fingers touched them lightly, turning each hand one way, then another so she could see how they were healing.

Lobo hesitated before moving again, as he intended. He had thought to be gone before she returned. But her touch was like a cool breeze against the skin of his hands, soothing the aching, burning rawness renewed by the physical effort. He was aware that several blisters had broken but had ignored the fact in his haste to finish the job and get the hell outta Newton. He had promised the boy, and there was no telling what the kid would do if the job wasn't completed, crazy as the idea was. Lobo was supposed to be getting the lot of them out of here, not helping them to stay. But there was something about the damned kid and those goddamn trusting eyes. Lobo wasn't about ready to admit to himself there was also something about the woman.

"Please come inside," Willow said. "I want to talk to you."

He hesitated. All he wanted was to make a fast getaway.

Instead, much to his own amazement, he found himself nodding curtly.

When they arrived in the kitchen, they found themselves followed by a trail of children. Willow grinned as she looked from one fascinated face to another, then chased them outside. "You too," she told Estelle, who was hovering protectively in the background. When all the curious ears were gone, she looked at him, her face solemn, her eyes searching.

"I have a proposition for you," she started.

One eyebrow arched.

"I . . ." she started, and hesitated.

The eyebrow went higher, but the eyes were as unreadable as always.

"I'd better see about those hands," she continued awkwardly, not sure at the moment whether she could present the offer she'd intended. He looked so forbidding.

"No need."

"But . . ."

"I've had worse burns," he said, in one of the longest sentences she'd heard from him.

"But not because of me," she countered.

"It wasn't you. I don't like to see animals wasted."

"And Brady . . ."

"If I'd known he started it, I would have left him there."

It was a flat condemning statement, and she winced at the harshness of it. Even if she suspected it wasn't true.

But his look challenged her to believe it. He was willing her to accept it.

His face was a study in cool indifference. It seemed impregnable until she remembered last night, the way he had looked at Chad before he had caught himself. There had been compassion in that look. Compassion and understanding. And Willow knew she had not imagined it.

The memory gave her courage. "I . . . we . . . were wondering if you . . . possibly needed . . . a job."

He glared at her with disbelief.

She hurried on. "I can't pay much, and there's not even a barn now to stay in, but you could sleep in the room with the boys and there would be meals and . . ."

And we need you. The words were unsaid but they hung in the air.

There was a flicker of amusement in his eyes, and then they went totally blank again as his mouth frowned. "You mean you really plan to stay. Lady, don't you have any sense?"

She looked momentarily wounded by his words. "I told you yesterday I had to stay."

He grated his teeth together in frustration before finally answering. "What about the kids? Don't you give a damn about them?"

"We took a vote last night. Everyone wants to stay."

"A vote?" Willow cringed slightly inside at the stunned disbelief in his voice. "Lady, you're as crazy as that damned bull of yours," he continued.

"Willow," she insisted. "My name is Willow."

He sighed heavily as if he were in the presence of a madwoman.

"Why did you fix the fence if you didn't think we would stay?" she asked suddenly.

Damned if he knew, he had to admit to

himself. The craziness must be contagious. Like cholera, and every bit as deadly. "I promised the boy," he said shortly. "I didn't want him trying it again. But for chrissakes, I thought you'd have sense enough to give up after all that's happened."

"That's why we need you," she said with the sweetest, most trusting smile he'd ever seen. It struck right to the core of his gut.

"Why are you so set on staying?" he finally asked. It was a question that had been gnawing at him.

"I'll tell you while I put salve on those hands," she said.

He glowered at her, his eyes hard and frosty. Finally he nodded, but with such reluctance that she suspected it was far more difficult for him to accept help than to climb down in a well full of rattlesnakes or drag a reluctant bull from a flaming barn.

"Sit down," she ordered, her head indicating a seat at the large kitchen table.

He surprised himself by obeying. He looked around the kitchen as she disappeared. There was a big pot on the stove from which an odd aroma came. His nose twitched, trying to identify the smells, but he could not.

The kitchen was cozy-looking, with flowered curtains and a colorful woven rug. There were numerous pictures, obviously drawn by children, on the wall, and pegs from which polished pans shone. The room was cluttered with books and clothes and pans, not neat like his room in Denver, but it was scrubbed bright and smelled clean and fresh. There was a feeling of warmth and comfort and . . . an odd blinding sense of coming home.

For a moment he allowed himself to wonder how it would feel to live in such a place, but he quickly dismissed the thought as being as crazy as the woman was. Even a hotel room soon became a prison to him after a few days; he could never stay long in one place. He needed only grass under him and a sky above. He needed spaces and freedom as he needed to breathe.

"Let me see them." Her voice jerked him back to reality, and surprisingly, particularly to him, he lifted his hands, palms up, to her.

"They'll never get well if you keep using them like that," she scolded, and her fingers ran over them, spreading cool, soothing salve on the raw areas.

He felt a curious weakness, a warm sensation that was becoming all too familiar when he was with her. The heat in his belly was bad enough, but the growing longing in his mind was even worse. He had never known a touch could be so light, so gentle. He had never known a woman's look could curl his insides. He'd never known the kind of weakness that settled in his limbs, one that kept him from pushing away when he knew that was exactly what he should do.

She looked rapt as she accomplished her task, all her attention on his hands, and he stole a glance at her. She was wearing a blue dress, simple but appealing with its small touches of lace. It was nearly the same color as her eyes, which were soft and concerned as she held one of his hands in hers while her other hand worked so gently. A tendril of dark auburn hair escaped from a twist in back of her head, falling against a lightly tanned face. She was all softness and warmth and beauty, and it scared the hell out of him.

"You were going to tell me why you want to stay," he said, more harshly than he intended.

She looked up, the blue eyes full of emotion. There was worry, and determination, and even a plea for understanding.

"If I leave," she said slowly, "this town will erupt into warfare."

He looked at her in amazement. Didn't she still understand what was going on? "It already has, lady," he said.

She shook her head. "Not like it will."

"And you're going to risk your life, and those kids' lives to prove that?"

"Alex won't hurt me. Not really."

"That's not what I hear."

"He won't," she insisted again. "And Jake trusted me to keep peace."

"Then he was a damned fool."

"And," she added with a stubborn look, "it's our home."

"It's only wood. Wood and nails. Rotting wood and nails, at that," he said roughly.

She shook her head. "It's the only home I've ever really had that's ever belonged to me."

He sighed with frustration. Reason obviously wasn't one of her strengths.

"You can't run this place on your own."

"That's why I need you," she said, with a quick smile that tugged uncomfortably at him.

"I'm not available."

"Why?"

Her hands had stopped working. One of them was resting on his, and he felt a jolt of electricity run through him, dizzying, tingling streaks of red-hot fire. "You can't afford me," he finally managed to say.

She looked at him, and he felt her appraising eyes, something that surprised him. "How much would I need to afford you?"

He wondered for a moment whether he should really tell her whom she was trying to hire, and what his usual fee was. It would be one way to jolt some sense into her. Yet he couldn't force himself to say the words. It sure as hell had never bothered him before.

"I don't plan to stay in town much longer," he said curtly, cutting off the conversation, and he stood up to leave. He saw her gaze move along the length of his body, resting for only a split second at his hip where the gunbelt rested, and then continue the perusal upward. His body seemed to turn to liquid heat as she did so, and he wondered how her body would feel next to his. It took all his will not to grab her and find out.

"You've seen the worst of the ranch," she said quietly. "We've lived here more than a year and we've not had any accidents until that first one when Sallie Sue fell. It's really a fine place. We just . . . need some help."

"You need more than 'some,'" he replied. "You need an army."

"I think you'd do just fine."

"Don't you ever give up, lady?"

"Willow," she said.

One of his hands went to the back of his neck. "You don't know anything about me."

"I know enough," she shot back. "I know you like children, that you're capable around the ranch, that you're very kind."

"Kind?" It was an expletive the way he said it. "Christ, lady, I thought—"

"Willow," she broke in. "Everyone calls me Willow,"

"I'm not everyone, damn it."

"No," she agreed evenly with a smile lurking on her mouth. His eyes, usually so cold, were now blazing. It was, she thought, very attractive. And dangerous.

"You're a lunatic . . . inviting a stranger into your home."

"You're not a stranger."

"I sure as hell am."

"If you meant us harm, you wouldn't protest so much," she said tranquilly.

He glowered at her, frustrated at her undeniable logic.

"At least stay for dinner," she attacked gently. "Although I must tell you Estelle cooked today."

He furrowed his brow. Things were moving much too quickly. He had never thought himself half-witted before, but he was quickly rejudging his ability to think, and cope, for chrissakes. "Estelle?" he said, grasping for time.

"She doesn't really cook so well, but we'd never tell her that," the woman . . . Willow . . . said. Hell, he was even beginning to think of her as Willow, despite all his attempts to the contrary.

"Why?"

The bluntness of the question made Willow smile again. He was obviously unused to sparing feelings or mincing words.

"Estelle has had a bad time," she said slowly, wanting him to understand. "She needs encouragement."

"And the boy?"

There it was again, Willow thought. That interest in Chad, although he tried to hide it.

"Him too," she said.

"And you?" He didn't know why he asked it. He certainly hadn't meant to. He wanted as little to do with her as possible. He wanted to know as little as possible.

She looked at him blankly for a moment, and his mouth tightened as he continued roughly. "What are you doing here? Trying to run a ranch on your own. You don't belong here."

Willow turned his own question on him. "Why?"

Because you're too soft, too innocent . . .

"This is harsh country, Miss Taylor."

Now *she* was frustrated. But at least Miss Taylor was better than "lady."

"Jess," she said, and it took Lobo a moment for him to realize she was referring to him. The name had a certain softness on her lips, and softness had never been a word applied to him.

He swallowed. He damned well liked the way the name sounded.

"Will you think about the job?"

"No."

Her eyes were wide, not pleading exactly, but expectant.

"I won't be here long enough," he repeated, not knowing exactly why he had. He didn't need to make excuses. He'd never made one before in his entire life.

"Will you at least have dinner with us? Chad would be so pleased."

Dinner with the houseful of lunatics! Yet the idea was suddenly terribly compelling. Part of him hungered to stay, but another part, the sensible part, warned him away. He already felt partially trapped. A few more moments, and he might as well surrender entirely. And she knew it. There was a gleam in her eye that told him so. He had the sudden feeling that she was not altogether as innocent as he had first believed. There was a sneaky streak somewhere in there. And he was damned determined he wasn't going to yield to it. Not to her. Not to the boy. He couldn't afford it.

He shook his head, pulled on his gloves, and rose.

"I have things to do," he said curtly, brushing beside her as she also rose from the table. But before she could make one more objection, his long legs had propelled him out the door, off the porch, and into the saddle. Without a backward glance, he spurred the pinto into a gallop, as if all the demons in hell were after him.

Lobo had killed his first man, the son of an Apache chief, at twelve, and he'd killed his first white man when he was sixteen. The soldier had been one of the few whites he'd seen close up since his capture eight years earlier; there had been several others, a few slaves who'd survived Apache initiation, and renegade traders who brought whiskey and guns into camp. But then most of them had been as much Apache as white.

Lobo had killed the white soldier for the simple reason the man had been trying to kill him. Lobo had felt no regret at the action, only a certain satisfaction that it was not him lying on the ground.

Other killings also came easily. He'd never formed attachments with anyone other than his brother. A human being, particularly one shooting at him, merited no more concern than a food animal, perhaps even less, for the latter was innocent.

The Apache were hard taskmasters and

tolerated no weakness. It was a lesson he'd learned well. But they did have their own code of justice and honor, and because of that he still lived today. . . .

Lobo slowed his pinto. If only she knew. If only she knew some of the things he'd done.

Christ, she would run like hell and never look back.

He pulled off one of his gloves, the salve making it sticky and uncomfortable. Damn. He rubbed it against his leg, and then against the back of his neck in unconscious motion. The woman and kids had no idea what they were involved in. Newton had said he was hiring more men. Marsh Canton was in town. The whole territory was ready to explode. He'd seen it before, and he could smell it coming now.

Lobo knew it was time to leave. He'd failed and he knew after today there was no way to frighten her and her family of misfits from the ranch. He also knew that he, particularly, had lost any ability to terrorize them, although he was realistic enough to know that Willow Taylor, like every other decent woman, would be horrified when she actually learned who he was. She wouldn't want to touch him, then. Not even to bandage a wound.

But he couldn't forget her plea. Or her words. Or those of the chubby little girl. "I like you."

His stomach clenched in agony. His head swam with uncertainty. Maybe . . .

But then he remembered the room, the

room full of books. He sure as hell didn't belong there. Books. A teacher. Things he'd never known.

Lobo thought of the humiliation of not being able to read, not even the telegrams that summoned him to do what he did best. The words had to be read to him by one of the few people he trusted in Denver. He could write his name but not much more. He could recognize denominations of bills, but he couldn't count them. He relied on his reputation to keep men from cheating him, that and clever ways he had devised to keep people from learning he couldn't read or write.

Lobo had wanted to learn. Not only wanted, but craved the independence and power he believed came with it. But he'd always been afraid of being laughed at, at seeing fear change to ridicule in faces around him.

And he had never learned to ask anyone for help.

Now he was getting weak-kneed about a woman who would despise a man of ignorance.

He swore every Apache curse and white oath he could remember. But none of it did any good.

THE EDITOR'S CORNER

What an irresistible line-up of romance reading you have coming your way next month. Truly, you're going to be **LOVESWEPT** by these stories that are guaranteed to heat your blood and keep you warm throughout the cold, winter days ahead.

First on the list is **WINTER BRIDE**, LOVESWEPT #522, by the ever-popular Iris Johansen. Ysabel Belfort would trade Jed Corbin anything for his help on a perilous mission—her return to her South American island home, to recover what she'd been forced to leave behind. But he demands her sensual surrender, arousing her with a fierce pleasure, until they're engulfed in a whirlwind of danger and desire. . . . A gripping and passionate love story, from one of the genre's premier authors.

You'll be **BEWITCHED** by Victoria Leigh's newest LOVESWEPT, #523, as Hank Alton is when he meets Sally. According to his son, who tried to steal her apples, she's a horribly ugly witch, but instead Hank discovers a reclusive enchantress whose eyes shimmer with warmth and mystery. A tragedy had sent Sally Michaels in search of privacy, but Hank shatters her loneliness with tender caresses and burning kisses. Victoria gives us a shining example of the power of love in this touching romance guaranteed to bring a smile to your face and tears to your eyes.

Judy Gill creates a **GOLDEN WARRIOR**, LOVESWEPT #524, in Eric Lind, for he's utterly masculine, outrageously sexy, and has a rake's reputation to match! But Sylvia Mathieson knows better than to get lost in his bluer-than-blue eyes. He claims to need the soothing fire of her love, and she aches to feel the heat of his body against hers, but could a pilot who roams the skies ever choose to make his home in her arms? The sensual battles these two engage in will keep you turning the pages of this fabulous story from Judy.

Please give a big welcome to brand-new author Diane Pershing and her first book, **SULTRY WHISPERS**, LOVESWEPT #525. Lucas Barabee makes Hannah Green melt as he woos her with hot lips and steamy embraces. But although she wants the job he offered, she knows only too well the danger of mixing business with pleasure. You'll delight in the sweet talk and irresistible moves Lucas must use to convince Hannah she can trust him with her heart. A wonderful romance by one of our New Faces of '92!

In **ISLAND LOVER**, LOVESWEPT #526, Patt Bucheister sweeps you away to romantic Hawaii, where hard-driving executive Judd Stafford has been forced to take a vacation. Still, nothing can distract him . . . until he meets Erin Callahan. Holding her is like riding a roller coaster of emotions—all ups and downs and stomach-twisting joy. But Erin has fought hard for her independence, and she isn't about to make it easy for Judd to win her over. This love story is a treat, from beginning to end!

Laura Taylor has given her hero quite a dilemma in **PROMISES**, LOVESWEPT #527. Josh Wyatt has traveled to the home he's never known, intending to refuse the inheritance his late grandfather has left him, but executor Megan Montgomery is determined to change his mind. A survivor and a loner all his life, Josh resists her efforts, but he can't ignore the inferno of need she arouses in him, the yearning to experience how it feels to be loved at last. Laura has outdone herself in crafting a story of immense emotional impact.

Look for four spectacular books this month from FAN-FARE. Bestselling author Nora Roberts will once again win your praise with **CARNAL INNOCENCE**, a riveting contemporary novel where Caroline Waverly learns that even in a sleepy town called Innocence, secrets have no place to hide, and in the heat of steamy summer night it takes only a single spark to ignite a deadly crime of passion. Lucy Kidd delivers **A ROSE WITHOUT THORNS**, a compelling historical romance set in eighteenth-century England. Susannah Bry's world is turned upside-down when her father sends her to England to live with wealthy relatives, and she meets the bold and dashing actor Nicholas Carrick. New author Alexandra Thorne will dazzle you with the contemporary novel **DESERT HEAT**. In a world of fiery beauty, lit by a scorching desert sun, three very different women will dare to seize their dreams of glory . . . and irresistible love. And, Suzanne Robinson will captivate you with **LADY GALLANT**, a thrilling historical romance in the bestselling tradition of Amanda Quick and Iris Johansen. A daring spy in Queen Mary's court, Eleanora Becket meets her match in Christian de Rivers, a lusty, sword-wielding rogue, who has his own secrets to keep, his own enemies to rout—and his own brand of vengeance for the wide-eyed beauty whom he loved too well. Four terrific books from FANFARE, where you'll find only the best in women's fiction.

Happy Reading!

With warmest wishes for a new year filled with the best things in life,

Nita Taublib

Nita Taublib
Associate Publisher / LOVESWEPT
Publishing Associate / FANFARE

Enter Loveswept's
Wedding Contest

AH! WEDDINGS! The joyous ritual we cherish in our hearts—the perfect ending to courtship. Brides in exquisite white gowns, flowers cascading from glorious bouquets, handsome men in finely tailored tuxedos, butterflies in stomachs, nervous laughter, music, tears, and smiles. . . . AH! WEDDINGS!! But not all weddings have a predictable storybook ending; sometimes they are much, much more—grooms who faint at the altar, the cherubic ring bearer who drops the band of gold in the lake to see if it will float, traffic jams that strand the bride miles from the church, or the gorgeous hunk of a best man who tempts the bride almost too far. . . . AGHH!! WEDDINGS!!!

LOVESWEPT is celebrating the joy of weddings with a contest for YOU. And true to LOVESWEPT's reputation for innovation, this contest will have THREE WINNERS. Each winner will receive a year of free LOVESWEPTs and the opportunity to discuss the winning story with a LOVESWEPT editor.

Here's the way it goes. We're looking for short wedding stories, real or from your creative imagination, that will fit in one of three categories:

1) THE MOST ROMANTIC WEDDING
2) THE FUNNIEST THING THAT EVER HAPPENED AT A WEDDING
3) THE WEDDING THAT ALMOST WASN'T

This will be LOVESWEPT's first contest in some time for writers and aspiring writers, and we are eagerly anticipating the discovery of some terrific stories. So start thinking about your favorite real-life wedding experiences—or the ones you always wished (or feared?) would happen. Put pen to paper or fingers to keyboard and tell us about those WEDDINGS (AH)!!

For prizes and rules, please see rules, which follow.

BANTAM LOVESWEPT WEDDING CONTEST
OFFICIAL RULES

1. *No purchase necessary.* Enter Bantam's LOVESWEPT WEDDING CONTEST by completing the Official Entry Form below (or handprinting the required information on a plain 3" x 5" card) and writing an original story (5–10 pages in length) about one of the following three subjects: (1) The Most Romantic Wedding, (2) The Funniest Thing That Ever Happened at a Wedding, or (3) The Wedding That Almost Wasn't. Each story must be typed, double spaced, on plain 8 1/2" x 11" paper, and must be headed on the top of the first page with your name, full address, home telephone number, date of birth, and, below that information, the title of the contest subject you selected when you wrote your story. You may enter a story in one, two, or all three contest categories, but a separate Entry Form or Card must accompany each entry, and each entry must be mailed to Bantam in a separate envelope bearing sufficient postage. Completed Entry Forms or Cards, along with your typed story, should be sent to:

   BANTAM BOOKS
   LOVESWEPT WEDDING CONTEST
   Department NT
   666 Fifth Avenue
   New York, New York 10103

   All stories become the property of Bantam Books upon entry, and none will be returned. All stories entered must be original stories that are the sole and exclusive property of the entrant.

2. *First Prizes (3).* Three stories will be selected by the LOVESWEPT editors as winners in the LOVESWEPT WEDDING CONTEST, one story on each subject. The prize to be awarded to the author of the story selected as the First Prize winner of each subject-matter category will be the opportunity to meet with a LOVESWEPT editor to discuss the story idea of the winning entry, as well as publishing opportunities with LOVESWEPT. This meeting will occur at either the Romance Writers of America convention to be held in Chicago in July 1992 or at Bantam's offices in New York City. Any travel and accommodations necessary for the meeting are the responsibility of the contest winners and will not be provided by Bantam, but the winners will be able to select whether they would rather meet in Chicago or New York. If any First Prize winner is unable to travel in order to meet with the editor, that winner will have an opportunity to have the First Prize discussion via an extended telephone conversation with a LOVESWEPT editor. The First Prize winners will also be sent all six LOVESWEPT titles every month for a year (approximate retail value: $200.00).

   Second Prizes (3). One runner-up in each subject-matter category will be sent all six LOVESWEPT titles every month for six months (approximate retail value: $100.00).

3. All completed entries must be postmarked and received by Bantam no later than January 15, 1992. Entrants must be over the age of 21 on the date of entry. Bantam is not responsible for lost or misdirected or incomplete entries. The stories entered in the contest will be judged by Bantam's LOVESWEPT editors, and the winners will be selected on the basis of the originality, creativity, and

writing ability shown in the stories. All of Bantam's decisions are final and binding. Winners will be notified on or about May 1, 1992. Winners have 30 days from date of notice in which to accept their prize award, or an alternative winner will be chosen. If there are insufficient entries or if, in the judges' sole opinion, no entry is suitable or adequately meets any given subject as described above, Bantam reserves the right not to declare a winner for either or both of the prizes in any particular subject-matter category. There will be no prize substitutions allowed and no promise of publication is implied by winning the contest.

4. Each winner will be required to sign an Affidavit of Eligibility and Promotional Release supplied by Bantam. Entering the contest constitutes permission for use of the winner's name, address, biographical data, likeness, and contest story for publicity and promotional purposes, with no additional compensation.

5. The contest is open to residents in the U.S. and Canada, excluding the Province of Quebec, and is void where prohibited by law. All federal and local regulations apply. Employees of Bantam Books, Bantam Doubleday Dell Publishing Group, Inc., their subsidiaries and affiliates, and their immediate family members are ineligible to enter. Taxes, if any, are the responsibility of the winners.

6. For a list of winners, available after June 15, 1992, send a self-addressed stamped envelope to WINNERS LIST, LOVESWEPT WEDDING CONTEST, Department NT, 666 Fifth Avenue, New York, New York 10103.

OFFICIAL ENTRY FORM

BANTAM BOOKS
LOVESWEPT WEDDING CONTEST
Department NT
666 Fifth Avenue
New York, New York 10103

NAME _____

ADDRESS _____

CITY _____ STATE _____ ZIP _____

HOME TELEPHONE NUMBER _____

DATE OF BIRTH _____

CONTEST SUBJECT FOR THIS STORY IS: _____

_____

SIGNATURE CONSENTING TO ENTRY _____

_____